TESTS

THE MEDIC

--- PULLING THREADS ---

Book Twelve

SHERYLL O'BRIEN

This is a work of fiction. All characters in this book are the product of an overactive imagination. Any businesses, organizations, places, events, and incidents are used fictionally. Any resemblance to a real person, living or dead, is a tremendous coincidence.

ISBN 978-1-939351-32-6

Printed in United States of America

Mom,

I looked in the mirror this morning
and saw your face.
I was surprised by how much I resemble you.
I am grateful that I do.

ACKNOWLEDGMENT

To the women I test each and every step
of the way toward publication:
Andria Flores
And
Nancy Pendleton.
You are my rocks.
You are rock stars.
Thank you,
a million times,
thank you.

A heartfelt thank you to my team:

Andria Flores ~ Editor extraordinaire.
Nancy Pendleton ~ Goddess of the publishing world.
Jessica Champion ~ Web designer and manager.
25 Hours Consulting
Daryl Bruinsma ~ Cover Design & Animation.

Testimonials

"One book will set the hook!" ~ Nancy Pendleton

"This avid reader predicts that Sheryll O'Brien will become your favorite author. She's mine." ~ Ruth S. Bodreau

"The characters draw you in immediately. You will worry, laugh, hope, and love right along with them." ~ Donna Eaton

"There is nothing sweeter than a Sunday morning coffee, a blanket, overcast skies, and a *Pulling Threads* novel." ~ Andria Flores

"Everything you'd want in a good book. Humor, romance, suspense and great characters! It even takes place by the ocean! Loved it." ~ Helena Green

"I could write a book about the wonderfulness of it all." ~ Faith Lavallee

"Hunks, humor, and heartache! What more could you ask for?" ~ Marjorie McCarthy

"*Bullet Bungalow* is a page turning family saga and then *Netti Barn* and *Cutters Cove* come along and add a whole lot of trauma to the drama." ~ Jessica O'Brien

"The most promising new author I've encountered in my publishing career!" ~ Jim P. - Woodwind Press

--- Pulling Threads ---

Bullet Bungalow
Netti Barn
Cutters Cove
They Run
They Hide
They Choose

PENOBSCOT BAY
A Rocco Fiancetti Incorporated Investigation

Reasons
Rescues
Resolutions
Torment
Tango
Tests

Coming soon…

Resolve
Revenge
Rebound

--- Twisted Threads ---

Coming soon…

Her Scream
Stay Safe

Malcolm

He stormed from their bedroom, down a hallway and through the adjoining space, dodging toolboxes, sawhorses, and construction debris left by a renovation crew. Walled off areas were starting to take shape — a nursery and playroom for his soon-to-be daughter — but nothing else in his life had shape anymore. **"Gretchen!"** the word echoed as he moved to the place where his wife had taken refuge. He balled the note she'd left and threw it from his hand.

The angry, advancing man stopped inches from the guest suite. He raised his fist to do some serious damage to the door — but lowered it when he realized that wasn't the barrier between them. Malcom unclenched his fist and placed his palm against the woodgrain. He lowered his head, his voice, "You need to set yourself right about me, Gretchen."

He turned and walked away.

Gretchen

She heard the tiny ping of the elevator seconds before she heard Malcolm call her name. When she didn't answer his call, she knew he'd check the bedroom and find the note she'd left on her pillow.

Malcolm, I need some time.
I've moved into the guest suite.
I hope you will respect my choice. Gretchen

The pregnant woman behind the closed door was staggered by her husband's building rage as he stormed through the penthouse – stunned by the heated emotion that owned the call of her name, **"Gretchen!"** It was all so unfamiliar. When she left the home they shared, she hoped her husband would give her the space she needed. She expected he would make his displeasure known – perhaps even demand she talk to him – listen to him.

She never thought he'd walk away.

Tests

Stacy Remington is dead.
Though her death is a tragedy—she is at peace.
Those who mourn her—
well, they may never know peace again.

Granger

Mr. and Mrs. Mitchell are in Philadelphia. They are not at their home on Old Estate Road; that residence is a crime scene and has been locked down by authorities. Granger and Faye are at their second home, a lovely 3,000 square foot condo the missus owned before marrying the man who is currently trudging a hole through her carpet. Occasional utterances of, "Plan…Wrong…No…" are heard as the mister passes by, but mostly, there is silence – heartbreaking silence.

It is a wonder the 65-year-old man is still upright, after all, he witnessed the death of his beloved Stacy, the woman he thinks of – thought of—as his daughter. The once powerful woman of furrowed brow, firm stance, and heavy foot, is no more. She was felled by an assassin's bullet meant for her father-figure. The woman of note was a great many things to a great many people, and over time she will be remembered as such, but the reality of this moment is quite simple:

Stacy Remington is nothing more than a corpse in a morgue at Philadelphia Hospital.

The Harvard Law graduate, noted scholar from both the John F. Kennedy School of Government, and the Massachusetts Institute of Technology, was the director of the Federal Investigative Cyber Agency (FICA), a division of the FBI. Twelve or so hours ago, the senior ranking agent was killed during a botched 'lure and capture' plan set to ensnarl a former Army Ranger turned paid assassin, known as Boston. In recent weeks, the killer had been systematically eliminating informants who'd turned against The Realm, a worldwide criminal organization thought by many to have been decimated. Something, or some things, recently happened to make Stacy Remington think otherwise about the status of The Realm. Fearing she was being surveilled by someone inside the Bureau, the director began working from home. On the down-low, she sought help from Rocco Fiancetti Incorporated (RFI), an elite group of gun-toting, cyber-hunting, karate-chopping, secret-snooping, criminal-catching men and women. Manuel Xavier, a former FBI subordinate of Director Remington, and current field detective with RFI, was one of the individuals who devised the 'lure and capture' plan and then took oversight of its execution. It's safe to say the plan was flawed—fatally flawed.

There will be a great deal of second-guessing, and what-iffing, and hand-wringing, and ass-kicking in the days and weeks to come. For all of the upcoming effort the final takeaway will be this: Director Remington did not need to be onsite for the operation. She was there because **he** was there. The **he** in reference is the man who is currently caught in a circuitous trek to nowhere and locked in a torturous recall of Stacy's murder…

"Come in, Stacy."

The director entered the Cottage on Old Estate Road, took a set of earbuds from Philadelphia Detective, Ted Brothers, who was cloaked in shadow at the front entrance of the Mitchell estate. She followed Granger Mitchell through a magnificent stone, steel, and glass foyer, halted her progression for a-fraction-of-a-fraction-of-a-second, reached out to touch him, to stop him, then shook off whatever IT was that nudged her, and continued on with the ruse.

"You have a name for me. Someone associated with The Realm?" she asked, playing her part, the supposed reason behind her trip from DC to Philly.

"I do."

They'd made it half-way into the kitchen when they stopped. The abrupt halt placed Granger in the crosshairs of the assassin lying in wait just beyond a wall of windows. A second, maybe two, passed. Stacy heard the ear-budded words of Steve Phelps, the RFI sniper set to shoot the paid assassin.

"He's ready for shot."

Those words were spoken in concert with Stacy's movement toward Granger—or maybe it was he who moved—the traumatized man can't remember. Yet he'll never forget the look of panic on her face, the pop of breaking glass, the sticky touch and sweet, metallic smell of blood, **her** blood…Stacy's blood. Granger reached his arm, Stacy fell against it, and the two went to the floor. He screamed her name…tried to stem the bleeding…felt her leave…heard the words.

"I'm sorry, sir. She's gone."

The stranger's utterance was in harmony with his own plaintive plea. "Stacy. Please. Stacy. No." Granger Mitchell, the man who loved Stacy Remington beyond measure, repeated her name until he could speak no more. "Stacy. Please. Stacy…please."

~

He had been in a hospital holding room with Stacy Remington – holding her hand and sharing tears of loss and regret when Detective Fred Serpico came to retrieve him. Granger placed a lengthy kiss on Stacy's hand; he would have preferred leaving that kiss on her forehead, but her injuries were… The shattered man righted himself with a deep breath and stood tall, "I love you, and I will miss you every day. No one has made me prouder than you have. You found that space in my heart that I had saved for you, only you, Stacy."

Attorney Granger Mitchell reached into his pocket, removed one of his business cards and tucked it into Stacy's hand. "I gave you one of these on the day we met. I told you that if you wrote to me I'd write back. There have been few things in this life of which I've been certain. Your writing to me was one of those things. You found my heart that day, Stacy. Seeing you here, like this, is breaking it."

Granger Mitchell gave one final kiss upon each of her fingers, folded them over his card, then walked away from the little girl from Harlem who grew up to become an incredible woman, one who made him a better man.

Faye Mitchell leaves the bottom step upon which she has been perched, takes hold of her husband's hand, and joins him on his silent death march through their condo. On their third pass through and around, he abruptly changes course and leads his wife upstairs where he hopes to rest his broken heart.

Shelby

FBI Director Webber is standing center aisle on a chartered jet awaiting takeoff from Philadelphia International Airport. She is dreadfully lost in thought. There are two reasons for Shelby's upright position: one, the jet has not been assigned a runway; and two, she is incapable of settling herself for more than a few seconds at a time. Her insides are a jumble of anxious energy, her thoughts disjointed in form. They travel at lightning speed from one set of circumstances to wholly unrelated snippets of this conversation or that interaction. Her usually well-trained, laser-focused headspace rambles about freely. She lets it, otherwise she'd be openly grieving the loss of her employee, her friend. "My friend," she acknowledges before finding **that** memory, the one from several years ago, the one that started their after-hours relationship…

Recently appointed FBI Director Shelby Webber was waiting for FICA Assistant Director Stacy Remington to join her for a meeting. The get-together was not taking place at J. Edgar—far from it, actually. Shelby Webber was at her Arlington, Virginia, waterfront home, treading a path across gleaming hardwood floors. Her pacing took her from corner to corner in front of floor to ceiling windows that overlooked the Potomac River. The director, so deep in thought, made no note of the view of the waterway she loved. Rather, she was considering and reconsidering what she was about to do. A beep from a security panel at the far end of the room announced her guest's arrival and signaled the end of her deliberation. "Showtime," Shelby said as she keyed in a twelve-digit code that activated a wrought iron security gate through which Remington drove.

The director jogged down a set of stairs and exited her home just as her subordinate exited her vehicle. The assistant director, a generally brusque woman **not** prone to displays of—anything—did what everyone did when they took in the stately nineteenth century brick home and beautiful Potomac that moved just beyond the shoreline. She gasped and gawked.

"Permission to speak freely, Director?"

"Yes. And for the next hour or so I would like you to address me as Shelby."

There was a n.o.t.i.c.e.a.b.l.e. p.a.u.s.e. followed by an unsure nod and raised brow, "Very well, Shellllbeee." Stacy swallowed that experience hard, "Well, that surely caused some internal discomfort, and I'm afraid it has displaced what I'd planned to say."

Shelby smiled wide, "I can imagine. I have a matter to discuss, AD Remington. It is a conversation that I will deny took place." She gave the woman a quick look then continued. "At this point in time, Stacy, there are four people who know about an issue. If word were to get out, a) I will know that you leaked the information, and b) covert assets will be unmasked. Take a few minutes to enjoy the view, and if you decide to assist with this matter, see yourself in."

Stacy didn't take the offered time. Rather, she followed Shelby inside the three-story home and into an expansive kitchen with a huge farmer's table.

"Take a seat." The director attended a waiting coffee percolator, while Stacy's eyes settled on a view of the Potomac through a wall of windows. "You take your coffee black, is that correct?"

"Yes, ma'am, Shelby, ma'am." Stacy shook her head, "It's going to take a minute to adjust, Shelby."

~

It was nearly 5 AM when the FBI director arrived at Pennsylvania Hospital. She wanted to go to Stacy Remington, but she went to the ICU to deal with Paul Ferraro.

"Former Agent Xavier, please update me on the events, post shootings."

"Within a minute of firing his rifle, the shooter of Stacy Remington, Paul Ferraro, was approached by RFI team members, Steve Phelps and Michael Monopoli. Phelps secured the firearm; Monopoli performed triage. No words were spoken to the downed man. RFI team member Fred Serpico arrived at the scene within minutes accompanied by EMTs, who had been on standby. Serpico read Mr. Ferraro his rights as witnessed by five individuals: two paramedics; Specialist Monopoli; RFI sniper, Steve Phelps; and myself. Serpico rode in the ambulance with Mr. Ferraro and remained inside the emergency treatment room while the patient was being worked on. Serpico accompanied the prisoner to the surgical unit and observed the patient during anesthetization. Serpico was waiting for Mr. Ferraro in the recovery area and followed him to ICU. Serpico remained with Mr. Ferraro until I arrived in the ICU. I read Mr. Ferraro his rights as witnessed by Serpico and medical personnel. I am requesting permission to remand Paul Ferraro aka Boston to the custody of the FBI."

"Granted. Thank you for your assistance in this matter, Mr. Xavier." The director of the FBI turned her attention to the prisoner, "Mr. Ferraro, you have the right to remain silent…"

~

"Stacy," the word caught on a pained exhale when she entered the hospital holding room. Shelby remained at the doorway unable to make her way to the deceased. A minute or so passed before she righted herself and moved forward. She stopped alongside the gurney and took hold of Stacy's hand; she found a business card inside her folded fingers. "Granger Mitchell," she read the name. "Granger," the name crushed with emotion. "This will kill him. He shouldn't have been there. You shouldn't have been there," she angrily addressed the deceased. Shelby Webber put Stacy's hand down, patted it several times, straightened her spine and walked away. "Goodbye, Director Remington."

Shelby reaches into her pocket and removes a business card. She holds it in shaking hands, runs a finger along the raised-embossed words, slides it back into her pocket, and pats it several times.

"Ma'am. Excuse me ma'am, we're about to taxi."

She offers a single nod to the crew cut agent who's approaching, takes her seat, and buckles in. As soon as its wheels up—so is she.

Headspace

Mike Monopoli, grounds specialist and sniper; Hannah Leavy, cyber huntress and intelligence analyst; and Manuel Xavier, field detective and cyber analyst, boarded the Rocco Fiancetti Incorporated jet at Fox Hollow airstrip in Lewisburg a handful of hours ago. They chose seats—nowhere near one another—stored their gear, sat their asses, and haven't spoken a single word since. That's because they are in conversation with the voices in their heads. Given the events of the past 24 hours, those conversations are brutally painful.

Mike…

He met up with Fred after he trekked the woods behind the Mitchell estate. "I took a series of pictures on my way through," he narrated as Fred checked the shots on Mike's cell. "The killer took some time in the woods marking a trail. He **did not** do that work on the night he killed Celia Brettenvue."

"Reflective tape?" Fred asked.

"Yeah. Small, folded strips of yellow tape are fastened to east-facing branches on inward approach spaced about 50' apart. The tree marking begins where you dropped me off and ends a few hundred feet from the property line. The strips were put at a level that suggests our killer is 6'2" give or take. The killer has been in those woods on multiple occasions and probably knows the route by memory now. Whoever he is, he's trained in ground traverse. Add to that the up close and personal strangulation of two women, I think we are dealing with ex-military."

Fred flipped through the pictures, again. "Why didn't he take the tape? It's evidence. Leaving it not only proves how he got to the Carriage House, but it might also provide forensics."

Mike leaned back against a counter and pulled a swig of water. "Maybe he plans on coming back."

"Well, fuck."

~

Mike locked his infrared scope onto Paul Ferraro aka Boston when he stepped inside the quarter-mile perimeter from the back of the estate. From that point on, Mike didn't take his eyes off his mark. The backup RFI shooter updated his team, "200 yards from fire sight." He and Steve Phelps, primary RFI shooter, trained their scopes on the assassin as he settled in, set his tripod, and secured his rifle.

Steve whispered, "He's mounted."

Boston took his binoculars and scanned the bottom floor of the Cottage, then the upstairs, then the bottom floor again. He lowered his hand a fraction of an inch, turned his head slightly to the left toward Steve, raised the viewers again, and scanned the woods, first in Mike's direction, then toward the Carriage House, then back to the Cottage. He put the binoculars aside, checked the time on his watch, went flat on his stomach, inched into place, sighted through his scope, and waited for visual on his victim.

Mike turned his attention away from Boston and toward the Cottage when he heard Granger greet Stacy. He watched them enter the kitchen and stop. Granger was facing the wall of windows; Stacy was to his right and facing him.

Steve whispered, "He's ready for shot…"

"Granger and Stacy, down!" Mike yelled.

~

The RFI team entered 275 Market Street through the back entrance. Mike demanded they assemble for a deconstruction of events. "I was watching inside the kitchen. Steve was watching the shooter. This is what I think went wrong."

A moan pushed from Steve, "Is this fucking necessary?"

"Necessary and protocol," Fred answered.

Mike continued. "Like the rest of us, Stacy could hear everything Steve was saying. My best guess is that after she heard Steve say the shooter was ready for the shot, she overplayed the moment, or had second thoughts about Granger being there, or something hit in Stacy's mind that made her move to protect him—she stepped toward Granger just as the shot was made."

"She stepped..." Mike runs the scene again. "Stacy was to Granger's right. She was facing him. She stepped. No. He stepped. Away from her. He stepped?" Mike closes his eyes and runs it again, and again, and again. "Granger was the one who moved. Maybe." After many minutes of looping the shit through his head, Mike pushes back in his seat.

"Fred was wrong. I don't have a handle on any of this," Mike whispers.

Leavy…

"Agent Leavy, I have designated you 2.0. You will be filling the vacancy left by former Special Agent Joy Ann Watts, now legally known as Mrs. Joy Fiancetti. Agent, you may speak freely."

"Director Remington, my status will be Dead On Assignment?"

"Unless you decline the assignment, Agent."

"No ma'am. I'm in."

"Very well. You will be doing your training at the off-site FICA location, Netti Barn located in Mayflower, Massachusetts. Your assignment is effective immediately. I have paired you with Special Agent John Maxwell. I will notify him of his role in your training. Agent, if you come close to breaking through Maxwell's defense systems, then by the beginning of next year you will be DOA 2.0."

"Yes, ma'am."

"Have a seat Agent Leavy."

The agent perched on the offered seat.

The director came from around her desk and took the seat next to Leavy. "I have an additional assignment for you. It concerns Special Agent Maxwell. FICA is in the midst of significant structural change. My predecessor is in Federal prison for crimes committed against the U.S., and the preeminent huntress, formerly known as DOA is no longer working for the Agency. This is **not** an appropriate time to lose the preeminent defender. I need him heading my defense team so I can put my attentions to cyber offense and rebuilding the reputation of FICA. Certain members of the Review Board were ready to cut Maxwell loose for his part in the 2015 Netti Farmhouse security breach and cover-up—a shortsighted decision in my mind. My vote against his dismissal was the tiebreaker. I used considerable capital backing Maxwell. If he were to break protocol again, the blowback will be directed at me. I want Special Agent John Maxwell monitored 24/7. You are to finagle your way into Netti Farmhouse and report to me regularly."

"For clarification, ma'am. You want me to spy on Special Agent John Maxwell?"

"Yes, Agent Leavy."

"To what line am I to take this, ma'am?"

"There is no line, Agent Leavy. As an agent of the FBI you will do…"

"Whatever it takes."

"Yes, Agent. Are you still onboard with the assignment?"

"Yes, ma'am."

~

She tossed and turned fitfully—the conversation they had over drinks circled round and round like a carousel. After many minutes of mental machinations, she dragged her ass out of bed and went downstairs. She tiptoed to his room and raised her hand to knock when he yanked open his door. She could tell he'd been as restless as she.

Heated waves of desire banged between them.

She used it to her advantage. "There's little doubt that you and I are going to sleep together at some point, Special Agent Maxwell, I was wondering if we could start the sleeping together tonight?" she casually tossed.

John stepped toward her and put his hand onto the back of her head. Her light green eyes sparkled with playful desire. He pulled her close and gave her a kiss that heralded his need. Leavy pulled a breath and moved forward, forcing the fully excited man to move backwards. Her steps were purposeful, and when they reached the edge of the bed, Leavy put her hands onto John's chest and pushed. Before hitting the mattress, he grabbed hold of her hands and pulled her on top of him. The woman in charge straddled the man and stared, long and strong.

"Has anyone ever told you that you look like…"

"Aaron Rodgers," he finished for her.

She laughed and shook her head. "Don't interrupt." She bent and kissed him. "Has anyone ever told you that you look like you're about to get laid *real good*?" Leavy pulled her tank over her head, released a clip from her freaky bun, and shook out her long tresses.

John spread his hands across her back and pulled her until they were chest to chest. In one swift move, he had the exquisitely built babe beneath him. He pulled her FBI boxer briefs down her legs and his down his. He groaned with desire as he entered her.

"An FBI agent does whatever it takes," Leavy whispers.

Manuel…

"Former Agent Xavier, this is Director Remington."

"Good morning, ma'am. RFI is ready to make an arrest in the Abigail Forrester and Celia Brettenvue murders, and the attempted murder of Penny Meehan."

"Who is your suspect?"

"Paul Ferraro, a highly decorated former Army Ranger…"

"I know who Paul Ferraro is. I know his wife, Felicity Ferraro, as well. She's an attorney at the law firm, Preston and Porter. Her clientele is exclusive to some heavy hitters in DC, including Senator Turner Rodgers. You'd better be sure, Manuel."

"We're 99% sure, give or take 1%, ma'am."

"If I had a penny…"

"Ma'am?"

"Your standard reply, Xavier, '99% sure.'"

"Yes, ma'am."

"Continue. What is your plan?"

"RFI can arrest Paul Ferraro outright, or you can be in on it, that's your call, ma'am. The arrest can be made at his home in Chevy Chase, Maryland, although there's no telling what events will unfold. He has a wife and four young children who live with him, so we would prefer to make the arrest elsewhere. Since he works from home, and his businesses are spread across the country, we would rather arrest him in Philadelphia, the location of his crimes."

"Is Mr. Ferraro expected back in Philadelphia?"

"We believe so, ma'am. We initiated a plan to lure him to the Granger Mitchell property on Old Estate Road. When Granger called you this morning, he put our plan into motion. I'm assuming that you know there isn't a name in Celia's files that connects Tango to The Realm, or if there is, we've yet to find it."

"Yes, Manuel, I figured that one out."

"Of course, ma'am. It's my understanding that you've been working from home, Director."

"Yes."

"Surveillance issues at J. Edgar, ma'am?"

"Yes."

"And at your home?"

"I've been scanning daily. Thus far, I'm keeping ahead of unwanted ears. I admit that I didn't scan this morning before my conversation with Granger."

"We were counting on that ma'am. John Maxwell tapped in to your phone this morning. Others were already tapped in, ma'am. Your conversation with Granger was overheard. We suspect the information has been shared with the appropriate people within The Realm. Now that your line is secure ma'am, I'll continue. We have a plan to get Paul Ferraro to come to us."

"Tell me about the plan."

~

Manuel stayed back at the penthouse reviewing the plan one more time with Granger and Malcolm. He answered their questions, and when it came time to fit Granger with Kevlar, shit got heavy.

Malcolm walked to the line of respectability with his father-in-law. "You should not be doing this. Something—everything—about this feels wrong."

Granger placed his hand onto Malcolm's shoulder, "Take care of Gretchen and Faye."

~

Manuel found a quiet place and ran the plan looking for holes, then gave his father a call.

"This is the plan; find the holes. Steve and Mike will be in the woods long before the meeting time of 10 PM. Steve will be set for his shot. Mike will be watching for Ferraro and communicating with Steve. Fred will be with me in the Carriage House. Ted Brothers will be on the first floor of Granger's house. Stacy will arrive at the front door, Granger will bring her through the house to the kitchen, which is a big room with one wall of windows that overlooks the forested area. Everyone except Granger will have audio and voice communication. Everyone will have Kevlar. And those who need it, will have night vision capability. Work it through, boss."

"No holes on the setup, son, but I do have thoughts. The hit is the primary objective; file retrieval is secondary. The assassin is highly motivated to make the kill before Granger has a chance to tell Stacy anything. Boston will be in his lair waiting for the first opportunity to shoot Attorney Mitchell. He'll want to eliminate his target before Stacy even arrives. That's the only way Boston can manage both objectives—silence Granger and get the files. Granger Mitchell needs to stay out of the kitchen, and out of the line of fire until the last possible moment. As for Director Remington, her foremost objective is the protection of Granger, but she has a mole in her organization. She will want Ferraro taken alive so he can lead her to her traitor. Her preferred outcome may not be achievable if we are to keep Granger Mitchell alive."

"Understood."

"As soon as the assassin readies for the shot, Steve should take his."

~

Manuel's cell disrupted the heavy silence around him. The heartbroken man answered with one word, "Papa."

Rocco endured his son's pain for a moment, then tried to pull him back. "Manuel, your plan was solid and well-thought. I talked to Mike and heard his assessment; you should try to hear his words from the place outside your grieving heart. Manuel, what happened to Stacy is not your fault."

"I was in charge of the operation. It is my fault."

Rocco intentionally pushed his son. "Perhaps it's Steve's fault. Instead of telling everyone the shooter was taking the shot, Steve could have taken his own."

Manuel raised his voice to his father, "Steve did **nothing** wrong. He was keeping us in the moment by informing us of the events on the ground!"

"Ah, you are willing to defend Steve's actions and take responsibility for his judgments, but you are not willing to defend yourself. For now, you can take solace that your team members are doing that for you. Manuel, you are my son and I know you will get to the truth of last night's events. I also know that the path you choose to get to the truth is yours to find."

"But it's Stacy," Manuel broke.

"Si, that is the real issue for you. She was your mentor, and she held an esteemed place in your life, rightfully so. That is a void that will stay with you. There is no point in trying to put your grief into a place where it makes sense. There is no such place and no point in trying to hurry it along; it lives within its own measure of time. You know I speak from experience. Son, I am standing today because I learned that working through grief is the only option. Come home, Manuel. Learn that for yourself."

"I'm 99% sure, give or take 1%, that I won't be working through any of this shit anytime soon," Manuel whispers.

All water, Joy.

The RFI jet is greeted at the back end of Halifax airport by the head of Rocco Fiancetti Incorporated. Three members of his team are on the jet. Each of them has been quietly processing a mission that went horribly sideways. Rocco pulls them in one by one for an embrace. He says nothing. Really, what can be said? They make the hour drive to a forested fortress known as The Compound, the place they have come to think of as home. Waiting their arrival are Joy Fiancetti and John Maxwell, both former FICA Special Agents who built the cyber division from the ground up under the oversight of the esteemed former director, now imprisoned, Roland Gaffney. As a Dead on Assignment cover agent, Joy had limited interface with Stacy Remington—hell, she had limited interface with everyone, but she knew of Remington's work and admired her tremendously. John, however, developed a relationship with the director toward the end of his tenure with the Agency, bare bones and strained as that relationship was…

He was standing at a bank of windows located in a fifth-floor conference room at J. Edgar Hoover in Washington, DC when a disturbance behind him demanded his immediate attention. He turned and came face to face with newly appointed FICA Director, Stacy Remington, a powerful woman with skin the color of coal, cropped close Afro, burnt-sienna eyes that told no stories, and a smile that—well, there was no smile.

"Special Agent Maxwell, take a seat. The Review Board considers the breach of security at Netti Farmhouse, by your daughter, Annie Mahoney-Maxwell, and your subsequent failure to report the incident, as a one-off infraction in an otherwise exemplary record of service. Further, the Board appreciates your well-documented and informed testimony in the Roland Gaffney matter. Let me bottom line this for you, Special Agent Maxwell: FICA cannot afford to lose its preeminent huntress and its preeminent defender at the same time. That played heavily in your favor with the Board. Having said that, the matter of DOA being in the hands of MI6 is of major consternation, and a matter with which we expect your assistance. Do you have any questions or additions, Special Agent?"

The initial relief John felt when he learned he would keep his job had come and gone. "I have one addition and one question, Director."

"Proceed."

"I have had no communication with Joy Ann Watts in months. I am unclear as to what assistance I can provide regarding DOA?"

"She is known as Mrs. Fiancetti now, Special Agent."

John smirked, shifted in his seat, and smirked again.

The Director was well aware of the storied relationship between John Maxwell and Joy Ann Watts and therefore *got* the smirk and the shift; she moved on without address. "As for your assistance, you will do whatever your government asks of you, Special Agent. Do you accept the terms as I have presented them?"

"Yes, Director Remington."

"Very well. There is further business. Please remain here." The Director stood and walked out of the conference room.

~

He handed his FBI badge and service revolver to Director Remington on December 1, ending his fifteen year association with the Bureau.

"Special Agent Maxwell, are you sure you want to resign your position? Perhaps a leave of absence is in order."

"Thank you, Director, but I need to make a permanent break."

"Very well." Recognizing the finality of his words, Stacy Remington did something she never did, she approached her Special Agent and shook his hand. "I wish you well, John, and fiat lux."

The Special Agent's smirk broke into a w.i.d.e. smile.

With that, former Special Agent John Maxwell, walked out of the FICA offices and J. Edgar Hoover for the last time.

~

He tapped on the panel and waited for Leavy to come from behind the wall of the safe room. He pulled her into his arms. "I'm a free man."

"Did Remington accept your resignation without pause?"

"There was a suggestion that I take a leave of absence before making it permanent. When I refused, she approached me, shook my hand, and wished me well."

Leavy nudged John for what she thought was a joke. "Nice one," she laughed.

"Not kidding, Leavy."

"Surprises keep coming, don't they?"

Joy placed her hand on John's forearm, "They're here." She gave his arm a tender squeeze, "Are you okay?"

"None of us are okay, but the returning members are worse off and are going to take this hard, especially Manuel."

"Are you okay with Manuel and Leavy ….. being here ….. being together?"

"All water, Joy."

"Good."

Leavy is the first out of the transport vehicle. John takes a step toward her and opens his arms which she immediately fills. He kisses the top of her head, “We’re good, so if you ever need me, find me.”

Leavy touches John's cheek where evidence of Manuel’s fisticuffs damage still lingers, “I’m sorry, John.” She moves to Joy and accepts her embrace. The two women hold hands as Rocco joins them.

Manuel has been standing on the far side of the vehicle watching the display between former lovers. He walks directly to John and extends his hand, “We good?”

John nods and shakes his team member’s hand, “None of that shit matters. I’m sorry for your loss, Manuel. If you need to talk, grab a few beers, and come find me.”

“Beers sure sound good, John.” Rocco joins the two, and taps Manuel’s shoulder. Father and son, and Joy and Leavy head inside the Main Cottage.

John stays back to have a private moment with Mike, the youngest man on the RFI team, “I heard you’ve been the team’s rock. Do you need to stay in that place, or do you need to deal?”

“I need to see Annie,” Mike says tightly.

“She’s moved you two into my old place.”

Annie Mahoney-Maxwell, the youngest female RFI team member, is waiting for Mike. The pixie-sized woman with waist-length, honey-blonde hair and gold-flecked, acorn-brown eyes, may be short in stature, but not in opinion or determination. To the world, Annie is a force to be reckoned with—to Mike, she is his Sweet Annie.

The emotionally strained and physically drained man drops his gear inside the front door, "Don't ask, just let me be with you."

Every time Annie lays eyes on Mike she falls a little harder and a lot deeper for the dark-haired man whose quirky smile crinkles the edges of his dark chocolate eyes. She crosses the room, steps into his arms, and accepts his embrace and his pain.

One last time.

Kitt Mahoney and Maura Putnam are in the kitchen of the Main Cottage when Joy and Leavy arrive. The returning specialist foregoes greetings. "I wasn't at the shooting. I was on protective duty for Penny Meehan, the woman who survived an assassination attempt by the contract killer, Paul Ferraro aka Boston. I was with the team for the deconstruction of events, though. I'm going to give it to you straight. Everyone there last night is seven ways to Sunday fucked up.

"I'll start with Manuel and Mike because they are here, and you will be bumping against them in short order. You should know where they are in their heads. On the surface, Mike is the rock of the team. He took control when they got back to 275 and made the RFI members sit through his deconstruction. His job at the Mitchell estate was to visually track Boston as he made his way through the woods. Once Boston was set in his lair, Mike turned his focus to the kitchen while Steve kept his focus on the shooter. Mike is the only RFI member who actually saw the shooting of Stacy Remington.

"His best guess is that after Stacy heard Steve's confirmation that the shooter was going to take the shot, she stepped in front of Granger, perhaps in an attempt to protect him. Mike said if Stacy hadn't moved, Granger would have been hit, but based on the trajectory of the bullet, it would have hit where he was Kevlar protected. Mike's bottom-line assessment is that the height difference between Granger and Stacy turned a potential chest shot for him into a fatal head shot for her."

Leavy reflects for a minute before continuing, "Manuel is busted up professionally and personally. He was responsible for the operation. He devised it, with input of course, but at the end of the day it was his operation. He is second-guessing every damn part of the plan, but he's mostly stuck on the decision to have Stacy onsite. There's going to be back and forth on this—there already is back and forth on this. Steve didn't think she should be there, but Stacy didn't want the operation to go down without her being there. That was probably as much a professional call as it was personal. Granger was, after all, her father-figure.

"On a personal level, and I can relate to this, Manuel is a mess over losing the director. She was not only his former boss, but she was one of the finest women either of us knew. Stacy mentored her agents with an unspoken and unbreakable belief in them, which helped all of us achieve things well outside our natural abilities. I think when Manuel remembers how highly Stacy thought of him, he will push through to the other side."

Leavy addresses Kitt, "Fred is straddling the line between Mike and Manuel. He is offering support, and seeking it for himself. He has been working closely with a detective out of the Philly PD named Ted Brothers. After Mike's deconstruction, Fred drove to Philly to spend some time with Ted. I don't know what took place, but I think it helped Fred some. When he got back to 275, he learned that Steve left the team and plans to stay away for a bit."

Leavy turns toward Maura, "Steve was the person in charge of the shooter. He'd sighted Boston from his post in a nearby tree, and had just told his team that Boston was taking the shot, but before he finished his words, the shooter got the jump on him and fired into the Cottage. Steve followed up with a direct hit to Ferraro. Steve was the only one who had the visuals of the whole ground event. There is no question that whatever happened, it is on a steady loop in his head, and he's dissecting the shit out of it all. Maura, I wish I could tell you how long it's going to take him to screw his head back on, but sadly I can't. I can tell you that Fred thinks he knows where Steve went. He plans on giving his partner some time, and then he's going to try to get him back."

Maura walks out.

Kitt follows her.

Joy goes to Leavy. She takes her face into her hands and locks eyes. "Tell me what you need, Leavy?"

The emotionally wounded woman's eyes fill with tears. She tries to drop her head, but Joy holds it steady. "Tell me what **you** need, Agent Leavy."

"I need to say goodbye to Stacy."

Joy nods, "RFI will go to the ends of the earth to be with Stacy Remington one last time."

Bullet Bungalow and …

Fred places a call when he's a few miles from the Mayflower town line. "Cluster, it's Fred."

"You in town, Detective?"

"I need some time at Bullet Bungalow," he offers tightly.

"Go on over. Do you want company?"

"What time are you off duty?"

"Seven, but covering for someone until 11 AM."

"I should be good until then. Is the key in the same place?"

"Yeah. Jane's out of town for the holiday, so you've got the place to yourself."

"Thanks." Fred is ready to end the call when Cluster asks, "You okay there by yourself, Fred?"

"Yeah."

Cluster finds Fred at the water's edge, "Been here long?"

"Long enough."

"You been inside, yet?"

"Nope."

"I'm heading in. You might want to do the same."

A good fire is burning in a double-sided fireplace when Fred gets inside. The push of heat against his near-frozen-self causes a full-out shake. The Sergeant directs the former MFPD detective to sit at the kitchen table, then heads up to the second floor. He rummages through things Kitt and Fred left behind when they moved out of Bullet Bungalow and to the Rocco Fiancetti Compound. He returns to the kitchen and tosses Fred a pair of jeans, a UMass sweatshirt, and everything else he needs, "Take a shower, get dressed, and come back for some food."

Fred follows Cluster's orders. When he returns there's a full plate of leftover meatloaf and a baked potato side with a Firestone Walker Pilsner set nearby.

"Sit and eat Fred. I already know about Stacy Remington. I nosed around a bit after you called. If you want to talk it through, I'll listen. If you want to work it through, I'll help."

"Just being at the bungalow has helped, Cluster. To be perfectly honest, I'm in Mayflower to help Steve." Fred raises his drink, "Some fucking help, huh?"

"You'll do," he laughs. "I figured that's why you came, so I asked Grant Spiel to drive by Steve's place. Your partner's there," Cluster confirms Fred's suspicion.

The men remain quiet while Fred eats. He raises his empty bottle, "Could use another." Cluster grabs the empties and gets two more. Fred pulls a swig, "So, we had a plan. As it turns out, it was a shit plan." He shakes his head and pulls another swig. "It was a 'lure and capture a contract killer' plan. It turned into a 'look over there, the director is fucking dead' plan. We had men in the woods, in a Cottage, and in a Carriage House." He stops. He shakes his head, "Jesus, that sounds fucking ridiculous.... And we had the best fucking sniper there is locked, loaded, and ready." Fred shoots a look at Cluster, "No offense intended sniper Cluster."

The Sergeant laughs, "None taken. Steve is the best, you can take that from the second best."

Fred salutes with his beer, "Anyway, within a fraction of a second, the assassin takes out Remington, and Steve takes out the assassin."

Cluster gets up from the table and moves to the kitchen windows. He takes a quick look at the ocean, then turns and leans back against the counter.

Fred reads the signs, "You want in?"

"Not yet."

Fred nods and continues, "Mike had eyes on the kitchen where Stacy Remington and Granger Mitchell had just entered. He's the only team member who actually saw the hit. His deconstruction of events suggests that Stacy stepped toward Granger when she heard Steve say the assassin was ready for the shot. I was listening in, and I heard Steve whisper those words, and almost simultaneously I heard Mike yell that Granger and Stacy were down."

"That quick? That close?"

"Yeah. It was over before Steve finished his sentence. My partner left 275 before we had a chance to talk. He's looping the events, I'm sure of it, it's how he works. He's looking for the thing that went wrong," Fred says before pulling a long sip.

"Or Steve knows what went wrong," the experienced sniper offers.

"Shit, Cluster. Steve. Does. Not. Fuck. Up."

The bear of a man shrugs his shoulders, "Not saying he fucked up. How long was Steve in position?"

"He was perched in a tree for a solid hour before Ferraro arrived, then spent another hour up, before the shit hit."

Cluster pulls his last sip before running it through. "Steve was in position for a couple of hours. He is ready to pull the trigger. He said a few words. Maybe the shooter heard him. Or maybe the shooter knew he had company long before then. Or maybe a damned squirrel stepped on a fucking twig and freaked the shooter. The possibilities are endless. The only person who knows what happened in his scope is Steve. And Fred, if he did do something to alert the shooter, there's no way Steve is walking away without the permanent stain of Stacy's blood on his hands."

Beaver Falls

Benton Brettenvue, now known as Benny Terrio, is tooling through Pennsylvania in a cherry red Chevy Camaro he boosted from Granger Mitchell's neighborhood the night his wife, Celia, met her maker, "Your maker was the devil," he laughs.

"What?" the banging hot, raven-haired, golden-eyed, bronze-skinned, Layne Osterman asks.

"Nothing. Just thinking about the family—my dead and buried family. Must be the holiday that's got me thinking of my dead beavers." He laughs louder and longer. "Hey, you want to stop for some turkey and fixings?"

"Sure," she leans forward and turns on the radio just in time for a breaking news story.

> **Stacy Remington, director of the Federal Investigative Cyber Agency of the FBI was killed in an accidental shooting at the home of Philadelphia Attorney Granger Mitchell. Few details are known about the circumstances surrounding the shooting, but Paul Ferraro, a former Army Ranger and owner of a successful chain of survivalist training centers has been arrested in connection with the shooting. Tune in for updates on the half-hour.**

Benny starts laughing—really laughing.

"What's so damned funny?"

He shrugs, "You're into that survivalist training stuff… You ever meet that Ferraro guy?"

This time it's Layne's turn to laugh, "That'd be like asking if you know the drunk on the corner because you both like whiskey." She taps his shoulder, "Let's grab some food, I'm starved."

Chevy Chase

The absolute **last thing** Felicity Ferraro wants to be doing is preparing Thanksgiving Dinner, but she has four young children, and they've been looking forward to the holiday for weeks. From the moment they wandered into her bedroom they've been alternating between watching televised parades and asking questions about their daddy.

"Where's Daddy? ……. Will he eat turkey with us? ……. Mommy, are you sad? ……. Is it because the turkey died? …"

Felicity shooed the little ones away with a promise to call them back to help fold dinner napkins. The few minutes of quiet she allowed herself was disrupted by the musical notes that announce breaking news. She slammed the oven door closed and raced to the den arriving before anything was said, but not before her children saw the face of their father on the television screen. She quickly turned off the set. They quickly started in.

"Mommy, that's Daddy ……. Daddy's on T.V. ……. Is he famous? ……. Put it back on! ……. Mommy put Daddy back on."

Felicity Ferraro forgot all about Thanksgiving dinner preparations. She sat on the den floor and gathered her four little ones onto her lap, ran her fingers through the hair of the two littlest ones and began, "Something happened. You aren't going to understand much of this, but Daddy won't be coming home."

"Ever?"

"I don't know."

"Where is Daddy? ……. Is he hurt?"

"Well, Daddy got a small boo-boo, but he is fine now. The thing is, there are some people who think Daddy might have done something wrong."

"Did he?"

"Maybe, but the people he's with will help him figure it all out. For right now, Daddy is where he needs to be."

"Can we go see him? ……. Can we bring him turkey? ……. And cranberries?"

Philadelphia Hospital

Paul Ferraro aka Boston is fucked up. His shoulder is blown to shit and he lost two fingers from a bullet from the gun of RFI shooter, Steve Phelps. The injured man has had surgery on both injuries, evidenced by heavy medical wrapping and taping to his arm and hand. One of his wrists is handcuffed to his hospital bed which pisses him off. He pulls at the cuff and yells at the two armed FBI agents standing guard inside his room, "Is this fucking necessary!?"

Crew cut agent #1 responds with a simple, "Fuck you."

Crew cut agent #2 adds on, "Make a fucking move—anything that suggests you're trying to make a break—and I'm gonna fucking fill your ass with lead. And I won't miss **my** mark."

Paul Ferraro offers his own, "Fuck you," then starts laughing —manically.

Minty's Shack

Steve Phelps' house is an old sea weathered wood structure that sits on a peninsula that disappears into a section of the Atlantic Ocean called The Cove. The setting is the most desolate place in Mayflower, and Steve loves it. He bought the ramshackle structure for a song and spent years breathing new life into it. The pride of his exterior work is a full wraparound deck, perfect for sun worshipping and star gazing. The interior has new everything including two full-sized, slack-ass recliners upon which the former MFPD detective is slacking his ass. Steve hears the blast of Seger tunes long before the approaching vehicle arrives. The man who is not receiving visitors calls from inside, "Fred, I'm not doing this. Not now."

Fred steps onto the porch.

"Fred, I'm serious. Not now." Steve lowers the recliner and storms out the door, "Fuck, Fred, listen to me."

"How about you listen to me, Steve. It wasn't your fault."

"You don't know shit, Fred. It was my fault."

Fred remains silent.

"I can't do this. Not now."

Fred stares hard at his best friend, "If not now, when?"

Steve walks to the other side of the deck and sets his sight on the horizon.

Fred follows several minutes later and finds his friend staring out at the ocean. "Did you make a sound that alerted the shooter?"

"Yes."

"You're sure?"

"No. I'm not sure of a fucking thing. I saw Boston sight them through the scope, I thought he was going to take the shot, then he lifted his head a fraction, and turned it to the left. He took the shot without sighting again. I must have made a noise. I made a noise."

Fred waits a second or two, "And?"

Steve's rage turns on Fred, "*And?* And Stacy's fucking dead. Shit Fred, what is this? Some sort of new age, voodoo-shit-questioning for the fucked up sniper?"

Fred moves into Steve's space, "No asshole, it's a 'what the fuck are you going to do about it now?' She's fucking dead, and you're fucking human, voodoo-shit."

Steve takes the last step left between them, "And you're fucking leaving."

"Yeah, Steve. I'm leaving Minty's. I'm leaving Massachusetts. I've got a woman I need tending to, so fuck you."

Could have. Should have.

Malcolm has been sitting, roaming, and brooding at Hufnagle Park since he left the home he shares with his wife. He keeps his eyes trained on the lighted windows in the guest suite. He's set his mind firmly on the conditions of his return home. "You need to get over your running, Gretchen. So long as you stay in that suite, I stay on the street." The angry and dejected man vowed when he left his home that he would not return until light filled the penthouse, a signal that she'd returned home. The 'cold to the bone' man sits on a bench for another hour, then heads to his mayoral office to spend the night.

Gretchen is behind closed doors, resting uncomfortably on a club chair, her swollen legs raised onto a cushioned ottoman. Her hand is resting on her baby bulge waiting for the dance-from-within that comes every day about this time. While she waits for happiness to abound, she tortures herself with the events that sent her to a very unhappy place…

She woke to a kiss on her cheek.

"Woman, I'm sorry to wake you, but RFI is making a move to arrest Boston that you need to know about."

"You're not involved, are you?"

Malcolm lifted his wife's wrist and placed his fingers onto her pulse point; it immediately picked up speed. "Woman, you need to slow your roll or I'm going to insist that you be kept in the dark."

She nodded.

He continued. "I'm not involved."

"Randy?" she asked.

"Granger," he answered.

Gretchen threw back the bedcovers, "Nope. Absolutely. Not. Going. To. Happen." She put her hand out for a hoist.

Malcolm ignored it, "Woman."

"Don't Woman me, Malcolm Price." He offered her his hand. She swatted it away and stayed put.

"Gretchen, stop," he growled.

Rage tears filled her eyes. She called beyond her husband, "Manuel Xavier, get your ass in here, now!"

Fred followed Manuel into the room, "I'm here as backup," he took a look at Gretchen and added, "or as a prosecution witness, depending greatly on how things play out."

"Good, the troublesome-twosome. Listen up, do whatever it is you need to do to get the bad guys, but keep my father out of it, is that clear?"

Gretchen was silenced by the shock of seeing Granger Mitchell filling the doorway, "Gretchen Rae Mitchell, **that** is enough."

"Daddy? When did you get here?"

"We arrived recently."

"We?"

Just then an arm and a waving hand appeared from around her father's back, "Good morning, Gretchen," Faye said.

"Oh, good Lord, you're all in on it. Well, I forbid it and that's the end of the discussion. If the RFI men and women want to go after the bad guys, I say Godspeed and please be careful, but they will not take my sixty-five-year-old father with them on their James Bond escapades. And Faye, I'd expect better of you. What on earth are you thinking letting Daddy entertain this nonsense?"

"Out!" Granger bellowed. "Everyone but the father of my unborn granddaughter, please leave this room, now."

A mini stampede bottlenecked the doorway as Manuel, Fred, and Faye scrambled to get out. Gretchen hoisted herself from her bed and stormed past her father and husband, "Since neither of you felt the need to include me **before** the life and death decisions were made, there is no need to include me now." She continued to the en suite and locked the door behind her.

Malcolm was waiting in the bedroom for his wife to emerge from the shower. She addressed him with a flattened edge of anger in her voice, "If you are concerned with upsetting me, then I suggest you leave."

"Gretchen, please talk to me."

"Please leave."

~

She stayed behind closed doors until the need for sustenance won the battle over petulance.

Her father was waiting for her in the kitchen. "Gretchen, there are dangers associated with tonight's plan, but there are dangers for me, Faye, McKay, and Randy already. We know things, or the people involved in Tango and The Realm think we know things. There was a murder on my property, Gretchen. There is no reason to think that the killer won't come back at some point—and every reason to think that he will. I am compelled to act. You do not have to agree with my actions, but I request that you support them, nonetheless."

She stepped into her father's arms, "Please Daddy, please do whatever it takes to come back safely. DelRae and I desperately need you."

Granger pulled his girl in and whispered, "I promise."

Gretchen waited on the leather couch overlooking Hufnagle Park while her father went to spend time with Faye. When it was time for goodbyes, she joined everyone at the elevator and embraced her father and Manuel. She graciously accepted their promises that they would return unharmed.

"Where is Fred?" she asked nervously.

"He went directly from the airport to Old Estate Road."

"Manuel, if time permits, please extend my apologies to Fred and express my desperate need that you all return safely."

When the doors closed and the sound of the descending elevator filled the space with dread, Gretchen returned to her bedroom without so much as a word to Malcolm, Faye, or Randy.

~

Malcolm knocked before entering the bedroom. He found his woman curled into a fetal position staring off into space. He went and sat on the floor next to her.

"Is it over?"

"Yes."

"Is everyone coming home alive?"

Malcolm wrapped his hand around her wrist and felt the thumping of her pulse.

"There is a casualty. Stacy Remington."

~

She entered the great room just as the privacy elevator door was closing with Malcolm and part of the RFI team inside. Her husband banged the door open button, "You need anything, Woman?"

"Just wanted to say goodbye and to wish everyone a happy holiday."

Four sets of eyes shared a look of confusion.

"Thanksgiving. It's tomorrow. I'm sure each of us has something to be thankful for." Gretchen stared blankly, then turned away, "Have a safe trip."

The mother-to-be is so gripped by sadness that she almost missed her baby's two-step. Happy tears try to push against her anguish—they fail miserably. "Oh, DelRae, Mommy is so .... so .... confused. I've made a mess out of things, and worst of all I feel things that bring me shame. I am so angry that people who share love and friendship with me ignored my needs and let my father jeopardize his safety. I am so angry at myself for accepting Stacy's death as a blessing—only for a minute, DelRae, but Daddy came home, and that is what I wanted, what I needed, and Stacy..." Gretchen falls apart a bit, then circles around, "And I'm sorry I walked away from your daddy, but I just needed space. I told him that, but he went and ratcheted all of this up by leaving. And he hasn't come back to me—to us." Fear begins to settle deep, but it doesn't budge her.

Clusterfuck

Fred swings by the bungalow to talk with David Cluster, "I'm leaving. I don't know what to tell you about Steve other than to say he's staying. Sorry to drop this mess in your lap, but you might be the best one to deal with it. Check on him Cluster, and keep me in the loop. Good news. Bad news. Any news."

"Will do. Take care of yourself, Fred."

Before leaving Massachusetts the detective places a call. He is surprised when it is answered, "Granger, it's Fred Serpico."

"I have Caller ID, Fred. What can I do for you?"

"Are you at the Cottage?"

"No."

"Do you mind if I head there, maybe spend the night at the Carriage House? I need to work, Granger, and I need to work there."

"I don't mind, Fred. In fact, I wouldn't mind if you burned the whole estate to the ground when you're done." With that Granger disconnects the call.

Fred gets back in the Jeep he borrowed from Ted Brothers, turns his Seger playlist to shuffle, sets the cruise control on 65, and heads to Philly. Eight hours later, he's sitting on Old Estate Road staring at the place where Stacy Remington was assassinated…

Fred headed to the airport from 275 Market Street to meet the RFI jet. He greeted his former MFPD partner, Steve Phelps, with a w.i.d.e. smile, "Damned good to see you, Steve." He helped load some gear into Janelle's Jeep, then headed to the Granger Mitchell estate.

Steve listened intently to the plan, asked a few questions, ran the logistics through his head, and opined, "We don't need the Director on-site. All we need to do is get Granger in place, let Boston set for his shot, and I'll take Boston out. Stacy Remington does not need to be inside."

"Remington doesn't want this to be an RFI only operation. With her there, we have an FBI witness. With Ted Brothers there, we have a Philly PD witness. And with Granger Mitchell there, we have our legal asses covered."

"Your call."

"Manuel's call."

"Noted. When do I meet up with Mike?"

"Half hour." Fred places a call, "Head over to Old Estate Road."

"That's when I **could** have shut it down…"

~

"I'm missing something." An energy, an uncertainty, rolled off Manuel when he and Fred were hunkered down at the Carriage House.

"Run it," Fred encouraged. "But do it quietly, and quickly. Boston is moving this way."

"You know the plan. It's solid. Right?"

"Yeah. So what's bothering you?"

"Don't know, but I feel it."

"Yeah. Me, too."

"That's when I **should** have shut it down, when Mike announced Boston's arrival."

Fred pulls himself from his thoughts and onto the driveway at the Carriage House. He grabs the Brettenvue files from the back of Janelle's Jeep, unlocks the house, deactivates the security system, and collapses on the couch. He takes his cell out and calls Kitt. It's after midnight, still, she answers on the first ring.

"You almost done?" she asks kindly.

"Almost. I'll be back after Stacy's funeral. Any idea when that is?"

"Saturday, 10 AM at Trinity Church in New York. Stacy's ashes will be kept by her grandmother and laid to rest with her when that time comes. The services are invitation only. The RFI team has been invited and will be there." Kitt chokes back some emotion.

"Kittridge, I'm sorry, but I need the time."

"Fred, we're good. Take what you need, I'll be here when you're ready. How's Steve?"

"Fucked up. He was fucked up when I found him. He was fucked up when I left him."

Kitt pulls a few shaky breaths, "Maura is starting to unravel a bit. Should I tell her you called?"

"No. I'll call Rocco tomorrow. He can decide what to do."

Kitt can tell Fred is ready to end the call, "Hey, Fred."

"Yeah, babe."

"Happy Thanksgiving."

"Happy Thanksgiving. Give our boy a kiss and keep my bed warm."

"Good night, Fred."

He lets her disconnect. It's sort of becoming their thing.

Boston. Boston. Boston.

Ted Bothers holds his Lucky Penny in his arms. Just after midnight and after several hours of finger touching in side by side recliners, Ted went in search of every pillow and soft thing he could find in his log cabin home. He rested his back against the arm of the couch and made an open V with his legs. He laid the pillows, blankets, and towels across his chest, hips and hard edge, and guided Penny into the space between his legs. She gently nestled her back into the puffy space and welcomed Ted's embrace.

Many minutes of silence suggests Penny has fallen asleep. She hasn't.

"Ted."

"Mmm."

"What was Stacy Remington like?"

"Don't know for sure, but I'd say she was badass. I spent a few hours with her at the homicide scenes of Abigail Forrester and Celia Brettenvue, and only seconds with her the other night…"

Penny waits for him to finish his sentence. When he doesn't she gives his hand a squeeze, "Where'd you go?"

"—she paused. Director Remington paused."

"What?"

"Give me a minute Penny, I've got to run something: She entered the foyer, took the earbuds, and followed Granger Mitchell. Five steps, she took five steps, then halted her progression. She reached out to touch Granger—she tried to stop him, there in the foyer. Why did she stop? Why did she go?"

Penny stroked his hand, "Do you think she had a premonition, or a second thought?"

"Not sure. I know she considered Granger her father-figure. Maybe she started fearing for him…"

"Or that female thing came over her."

"Come again, Lucky."

"I subscribe to the notion that individuals of the female persuasion have this thing—call it intuition or whatever. I had it once when I was a little kid, and I had it the night I got shot. I knew I was in danger, sitting there on my own damned couch, behind closed doors, and I **knew** someone wanted to hurt me. I don't doubt for a single second, that if Stacy Remington paused, there was a reason. She probably knew. The thing is women get the sense that something's wrong, but they second-guess themselves. They ignore it, or push past it, and that is always the downfall of women."

Many minutes of silence suggests Penny has fallen asleep. She has, and it's a fitful sleep…

She readied herself for **the** conversation with Fred.

"Can I get you anything?"

"I'm good, Fred."

"No, not yet, but you're getting there," he smiled. "I'd like you to tell me what you told Ted about Boston, if you're able."

Penny nodded, then struggled through, "I got a sketchy vibe from Boston from the get-go. He said he thought he recognized me because I look military. I introduced myself as Staff Sergeant SSG Penelope Meehan, Army Reserves, and he said he was Paul Boston, Marine through and through." She was already shaking her head when her good hand got into the action by squeezing her pantleg. "My red flag first went up when he didn't introduce himself with his rank—it started waving full-out as our meeting continued. I've been Army Reserves for years and have been around Army men long enough to know one when I see one. My gut was telling me that Paul Boston **was not** Marines. My gut was proven right when he reached across the lunch counter for his soda, and I saw two yellow trimmed points of a tattoo peeking out from under his cuffed-back button-down shirt. The points are unmistakably part of an Army star tattoo. I have that same tattoo, so I'm 100% sure he's Army and not Marines."

Fred offered her a Serpico smile and encouraged her on, "You're doing great, Penny. Continue, unless you need a break."

She continued. "As for the shooting, I'd been home for a couple hours, had taken a shower, had straightened the place, and was on my couch reading and waiting for Ted. I was having trouble concentrating—I had a feeling something wasn't right with my place. No matter how hard I tried to concentrate, I just couldn't shake the feeling. Something caught my eye at the front window—a flash—a movement—a reflection from behind—I don't know what, but I had a split-second thought that must have registered in me as fear, because I started a right-hand dive onto the couch. I know there wasn't much time between the instinct to dive and my being shot, but in that space of time I knew the shooter was the guy from the diner."

Whenever Penny stirs or wakes, it's with a start and one word tumbling over and over, "Boston. Boston. Boston."

Ted whispers against her cheek, "I've got you, Lucky," then he trails kisses along that cheek and hugs her as best he can. She responds to his words, his kisses, his embrace with a sigh of contentment, and a squeeze of their clasped hands.

Channeling the judge.

Randy is perched on the leather couch looking out at Hufnagle Park when Gretchen enters the penthouse early Friday morning. She rolls her eyes and turns to leave when she sees him.

"Gretchen, I have a few things to say, and I'd appreciate your ear."

She turns on a dime, "Did you just call me Gretchen?"

"I believe I did. I'm channeling my father the judge, so if you don't mind, I'd like to get this over with as soon as humanly possible."

She bypasses him on her way to the kitchen, "I'm not up for a conversation."

"Good, because I'm the only one here, and I'm not interested in hearing what you have to say."

Gretchen stops, folds her arms over her baby ball, and begins tapping her toes.

Randy waits until she looks at him, "I'm not usually one to impose into the relations of others—"

Gretchen interrupts, "You should adhere to that position."

Randy snaps at her, "You need to listen up. Whatever you **think** you know about the 'lure and cap that turned to crap' plan, I can assure you that you are 100% wrong. I was there when the team and your father were devising. The Legal Beagle heard the plan then took over. He insisted that something be done." Randy lets his words sit and waits for Gretchen to run them through.

"Why did my father push for this?"

"You can't be serious. Celia and Dominique, two women he was in consultation with were murdered. Celia was murdered on his property where his wife was sleeping. Dominique was murdered in a solitary confinement cell in a federal penitentiary. People skilled in deadly deeding pulled off these dastardly deeds, for sure. More to the point, his only daughter recently had a 'don't stop' contract put on her head, and was present during two home invasions, one that resulted in the death of a felon and the other in the shooting of a police captain. It is also worth mentioning that the Legal Beagle's favorite employee, yours truly, was chased through the hallowed halls of his legal office by two gun-waving, mask-wearing, file-absconders. Your father was at his wits end with all of this, Gretchen."

"Still, he's a sixty-five-year old man, and he's my father."

"That was the point Malcolm tried to make," Randy says with a smile.

"Did you just call my husband, Malcolm?"

"Again, channeling the judge. With due respect, Gretchen, your husband hasn't been home for the better part of three days. He hasn't had the pleasure of your company—nor the favor of your willingness to listen to him—in more days than that."

Randy's words cut deep. Tears spring and begin to fall.

"Gretchen, that man pushed back against the planning forces. He challenged your father in ways I never thought I'd see. Things were said, ultimatums were made, and a few pleadings on your behalf were offered by the man of all men, Malcolm Price, who stripped himself bare for his woman. When Malcolm told you what was going to happen, and you went all blonde bitchiness and shut the man out, he got in Manuel's face and said, 'This fucking plan of yours better end with Granger in one piece.' I thought fists might be thrown between the two."

Gretchen walks past Randy and takes a seat on the living room couch. "Oh, Randy, what have I done?"

"Geez, Mrs. Mayor, you did what you always do—what Mr. Mayor always asks you not to do—you ran. I know you were track and field in college, but still it's a ponderance that you run. I've heard about the formidable Gretchen Mitchell ripping to shreds anyone who stands in her way in the legal arena, but when it comes to your personal battles, you fold like an accordion file. What up with that?"

Before Gretchen can answer, she feels a swift kick from DelRae. She bends over, "Ow."

Randy moves to her, "Are you alright?"

Gretchen nods, "I think DelRae is pissed at me, and she just let me know with a hearty kick."

"Yeah, well, she's gonna be a Daddy's girl, so you'd better get back in his good graces, or you'll be seeing your daughter every Wednesday and every other weekend."

Gretchen wipes a few tears and nods. She awkwardly pulls herself from the couch and heads to the kitchen. She asks over her shoulder, "Are you about finished with me, Randy, because I'm in desperate need of some food."

"You're in desperate need of a lot of things, Mrs. Mayor. We can start with food. Researcher Randy will get you sustenance; go take a load off."

And with that, the judge leaves, and The Kid returns.

A belated day of Thanks.

Malcolm is watching 275 from a bench in Hufnagle Park. He takes a measure of comfort knowing his wife isn't alone in the sprawling penthouse, but little else soothes the pain of their separation. His heart picks up speed when she comes into view. He straightens himself and trains his eyes on Gretchen as she paces back and forth in front of the guest suite windows then stops to use her cell. He ignores the incoming call. He doesn't know why she's calling, but he knows she's calling from her place of refuge. "I want you back in our home, and until you are…" The sentence goes unfinished.

Gretchen disconnects from Malcolm without leaving a voicemail. She immediately places a call to the other man in her life, "Hi, Daddy. I should have called yesterday."

"Yes, well, the same could be said here. Happy Thanksgiving, Gretchen."

"Are you and Faye ……. are you ……. well?"

"Faye is a great comfort, but I'm not sure what I am, Gretchen. How are you and the baby and Malcolm?"

"We're all ……. well. I'm sorry. I think I should ……. Daddy, I think I'm in need of a nap, please give my best to Faye, and stay ……. well."

"One thing before you go. Fred Serpico is staying at the Carriage House and working from there. I thought you'd like to know."

"Thank you for saying so. I really do owe Fred a call. I love you, Daddy."

"That pleases me, Gretchen. Our best to Malcolm."

"Bye, Daddy."

Before she invests a second of thought she makes another call, "Fred, it's Gretchen."

"I have caller ID. I answered it anyway," he jokes.

"Fred, I'm calling to apologize for my behavior. I was rude and thoughtless, and I am so very sorry for the way I acted. I am heartbroken for you, for all of you," Gretchen breaks on the last few words.

"Gretchen, I appreciate your calling, but you and I are good. How about you and Malcolm?"

She falls apart and stays apart for many minutes. He waits silently for her to pull it together. "He left. I drove him away," she says before breaking, again.

"Do you need me to come be with you?"

The busted up woman manages a short answer, "No, Fred, but thank you." She ends the call and curls up on the guest bed, where she cries herself to sleep.

Carriage House

Fred heads to the kitchen and pours himself another black and white. After his call with Kitt the night before, he did what he hadn't done during the previous 36 hours: he slept. The thing is it was a tortured sleep. Mike's and Steve's words—**Granger and Stacy down. Shooter down. MOVE. MOVE. MOVE!**—banged like a drum, then abruptly silenced, so a tumble of questions, mounting questions, could take center stage. He's been up for hours, plowing back brew and pushing through pages of notes Granger kept on the Brettenvue women. When he tired of the mind-meld, he went trudging through the woods and stood at the perimeter of the fire sight the cold-blooded killer used to end a life.

When he's had enough of it all he gives Ted Brothers a call. "I'm in Philly. Are you and Penny up for company?"

"If you can be here within the next half-hour, you can join us for a belated Thanksgiving dinner."

"Set a plate."

Drexel Hill

Fred arrives with what looks like a sizeable bouquet of flowers. It's really five bouquets he picked up at a corner minimart and bundled together. He presents them to Penny, who is on her feet and greeting him at the door.

"Well, look at you, shiny as a new Penny," Fred winks.

"I managed a shower, that's where the shiny comes from," she winks back. "These are beautiful. Thank you. Come on in. Ted's destroying the kitchen."

Fred and Penny crack up at the array of mixing bowls, measuring cups, stirring utensils, and pots and pans that are sprawled across the stovetop and counter.

"Not a word from either of you," Ted growls, "and Fred, you're on clean-up."

"Should have brought my damned overnight duffle, this is gonna take some time," he laughs big.

The Compound

Annie Mahoney-Maxwell spent all day in the kitchen preparing a belated Thanksgiving dinner. Rocco Fiancetti sent an earlier invitation. Sort of: **Attendance is mandatory.**

Mike and Manuel arrived at the Main Cottage early to move the great room furniture to the side. "Now, what?" Manuel asks.

"We get the table and chairs."

"We have tables and chairs? Like banquet shit?"

"Just like it."

As soon as the tables are up, Kitt and Joy put out table linens and such, while Leavy and Maura feed, burp, and change the little ones.

Callie and Tess, who have been assigned cleanup duty, stay out of the fray.

Rocco and John arrive from the lower level office just as Mike is hauling a beautifully browned and generously stuffed twenty-seven pound bird from the oven. He lifts it from the pan and puts it onto an enormous platter that Annie quickly garnishes with greens, sliced apples, and butter-sugar walnuts. Mike takes the picture-worthy platter to a side carving and serving station.

"Okay, everyone," Annie calls from the kitchen. "Grab a side dish from the kitchen and put it on the table with the bird."

Once everyone has settled at the table, Rocco offers a few words, "I am of a thankful heart that we are here. We should remember that others, who are elsewhere, are where they need to be." He squeezes the hands of Kitt and Maura who stand next to him.

Kitt squeezes back.

Maura slides her hand away.

After dessert and coffee, Rocco asks Maura to join him in the office. The cerise-haired beauty is somewhat edgy and feisty on a good day; this is not a good day. "I have babies to attend, Rocco, so put me in my place and be done with it."

The man is cut to the quick, "Maura, there is no place for any woman, certainly not for a woman of your substance. This side of you is of a fearful one. Your strength is found in the helping and healing of others. You want to help and heal your man. And you think you have been abandoned." He waits for rebuttal before continuing. "Your man has not abandoned you, Maura, he has abandoned himself. He is wracked with doubt, and he should be."

Maura turns hurtful defensive eyes toward Rocco.

"Ah, the woman in love with her man is back, and she wants to defend him. I am not diminishing the Rambling One in any way. I am telling you this: when men fail, or when they think they have failed, they pull apart every piece of their action and themselves." He gives her a moment. "My dear Flowering One, you are a brilliant physician's assistant, so let me put this into terms you can understand best. In order to see what's wrong with a patient you may need to look inside. You x-ray or scan or perform surgery to find what's wrong so you can fix it. When you go through the process of finding and fixing, the patient heals. If you don't find what's wrong, nothing gets fixed and the patient suffers and never heals. That is what Steve is doing. He is looking inside to see what went wrong so he can fix it and then heal from it. He is not running. He is not hiding. He is not abandoning."

Rocco loses Maura to tears. He pulls her to him and accepts her pain.

Back home. Sort of.

Randy knocks on the guest suite door, "There's Thanksgiving dinner in the refrigerator for you and DelRae. Try to eat something."

An hour passes before Gretchen pulls herself from bed. It's dark so she turns on lights, goes to the windows, and pulls the shades.

Malcolm lowers his head when he sees light coming from the guest suite. Smiles for a second when he catches a glimpse of his woman, all baby belly round—loses that smile when she shuts the shades. The man is cold, hurt, and fighting the pull of resignation that he and Gretchen won't set themselves right. He puts his elbows to his knees and lowers his head. He reconsiders his plan to stay away—thinks about going back—steels himself. "No. She needs to find her own way back this time." A light catches his eye—a light from the living room of their place—he leans back against the bench and waits.

Gretchen begins pacing in front of the windows overlooking Hufnagle Park. She paces for several minutes, it is a labored stroll. One of her hands is pressing against her low back, the other gently patting her baby, their baby.

Malcolm follows her every move. He wills her to sit on the couch and rest. She does. She nestles into the corner and pulls her legs up, staring blankly out into the darkness of Hufnagel. Movement to the left catches her eye. She leans forward just as a man moves toward a streetlight and leans against it.

"Malcolm." Gretchen pulls herself from the couch, steps to the window, and places her hand onto the cold glass. She begins to cry.

He watches. He waits. He hates seeing her pain, but hates it even more that she doesn't stay and fight for him, for them.

Gretchen walks away from the window, then reappears. She gestures toward the ground—the garage door begins to open. She is mimicking his actions the night she first came to him.

Malcolm looks up at the window. He smiles, nods, and begins walking home.

It isn't the homecoming Gretchen hoped for. Her man steps off the privacy elevator and leans back against the brick wall closest to its door. "We need to talk, Gretchen. If you weren't carrying our child, I would be doing the talking, and it would be on the loud side. I will hold my tongue, but you need to tell me why you keep running from me, from us."

"I don't know."

"Well, you better figure it out." Malcolm waits out a protracted silence.

Gretchen struggles to fill it. She begins pacing like a caged animal, stops on occasion as though she is ready to say something, then begins pacing again.

Malcolm knows she's lawyering herself, asking questions, probing deeper. **He knows** why she runs, but he needs her to know so she'll stop.

"Are you finished?" Malcolm asks.

"Finished?"

"Woman, you know why you keep running. Say it, already."

"I'm afraid to fight for us. I'm afraid you won't like the way I fight. I'm a lawyer, I've been trained to ignore emotion when battling. If I fight you, really fight you, get down into the feelings of it all, my emotional buttons will be pushed—I *can't go there*, I don't even know how to go there."

"Talk to me, Gretchen."

She begins pacing again. "The first time I ran from you it was because you manipulated me. I know you did it because you were trying to protect me from Cappa Escobar, and you were right to try, but I was blinded by anger, so I left. The second time I ran it was because you kept important things about your life with Sage from me. I thought that we were dealing in complete honesty when we talked about our lives. So, when we started talking about Sage that night, it felt as though you were only doing so because you had to because outside circumstances were forcing you. And this time, I ran because you sided against me on something vitally important."

"No."

"That's what I thought, Malcolm." She takes a step toward him, then stops. Something snaps in her and she turns the tables. "You know, Mr. Price, you stand there expecting me to take all this on myself. The truth is that I run because it's my response to **your** actions. I don't take kindly to manipulation, or lies of omission, or disloyalty. And furthermore, where the hell have you been for the last few days? I believe there's been some running being done on your part." By the time her burst of anger is over, Gretchen's arms are folded across the top of her baby ball and the toes of one foot are tapping.

"So, you **can** fight. Good to know, Woman. I don't know much of anything right now, but you can bet your ass that I'm gonna do things that will piss you off. I don't know what your boundaries are, so you have to tell me when I cross them—just like I'm gonna do with you right now: Don't leave our bed or our home again. If you want me, if you want us, then stay and fight. If you leave me again, Gretchen, I won't be coming back." Malcolm waits until his woman unfolds her arms and stops her pissy-toe-tapping before pushing himself off the wall. He walks to her, offers her his gigantic paw, "Come on, let's get your things from the guest suite."

For the next several hours the husband and wife pass one another through the space they call home. There are few words and no touches, but they are together. They nibble on the Thanksgiving dinner Randy brought home and share a piece of apple pie. When they crawl into bed, they don't find their way into each other's arms.

Gretchen and Malcolm may be under the same roof, but they haven't found their way home.

The Body

The Body is at his DC home. He is seated on a gray Queen Anne wing-back, leather chair set near a crackling fire. Two fingers of a poured, but not yet sipped, Woodwind Reserve bourbon rests on a nearby table. The man's legs are stretched out on a thickly padded ottoman, his hands are clasped and resting on his chest, his two thumbs tapping together in a sequential beat: *tap, tap, tap, pause, tap, tap, tap, pause*. The contemplative figure in the quiet, dark room is celebrating his successes when he pushes from his chair, "Music."

He goes to his sound system, talks to the space around him. "Celebrations need music. Vivaldi, *The Four Seasons*," he quickly decides. He is seated when the first notes of *Spring* begin. He raises his glass in toast, **"When they fall silent, Abigail."** He takes a long pull of bourbon and waits for the musical change. And when *Summer* begins he offers a second toast, **"Under the merciless sun, Celia."** He enjoys another sip and waits some more. And when *Autumn* begins, so too another toast, **"They find their pleasure, Dominique."** He finishes his drink before the opening strings of *Winter* fill the room. Lifting the cut-crystal decanter set on a nearby table, he pours himself two fingers of the copper-colored, 123.6 proof drink, raises his glass high and offers his final toast, **"And fall down to the ground, Stacy."** He drains his second glass in one gulp.

The Body recites his pieced together tribute to Abigail, Celia, Dominique, and Stacy. **"When they fall silent, under the merciless sun, they find their pleasure, and fall down to the ground."** He closes his eyes with a broad smile on his face and lets the music command his thoughts.

Going home.

Trinity Church near Wall Street and Broadway is an historic parish church in the Episcopal Diocese of New York. For more than 300 years, the church has stood with her City through significant moments in history. Today it will bear witness to the funeral mass of a most significant woman.

Fred greets the RFI team outside the church with handshakes and shoulder slaps for the men and cheek kisses and hugs for the women. Although he did not expect to see Steve this morning, he feels a ping of disappointment and a pong of concern at his absence. Within minutes of the team's arrival, a distinguished African American man of about fifty approaches and introduces himself as Mathis Reynolds, a lawyer and a friend of Stacy Remington.

He shakes hands all around then addresses Manuel, "Mr. Xavier, Director Remington asked me to give you something in the event she lost her life."

The words hit Manuel like a sucker punch.

Mr. Reynolds ignores the detective's discomfort and continues on. He hands Manuel a set of keys and one of Stacy's business cards. "Director Remington's property has been sealed by her next of kin. I informed members of her family that she did not want anyone other than you and Fred Serpico to have access to her residence, to her files and to her computer. On the back of the business card are her access codes."

Manuel flips the card and recognizes Stacy's handwriting, "When did the Director give you these things and her instructions."

"When I dropped her off at the airport that night. Mr. Xavier, Stacy *did not* have a premonition, or a doubt of you or your plan. The transfer of her keys and access codes was standard operating procedure when she went on a field assignment. She did make note, before going to Old Estate Road, that the work she had already completed should be given to you. She believed it would help as you work through your investigation. She asked that I say the following words: 'she was 99% sure, give or take 1%, that you were the finest young agent with whom she had ever worked.'" Mr. Reynolds smiles and taps Manuel on his shoulder, "I believe you are familiar with those words."

Manuel hangs his head.

Mathis waits, then brings Manuel back from his thoughts, "I hope you will get to Stacy's townhouse within the next day or so. Others are chomping at the bit to get inside and see what's there." With that Mr. Reynolds walks away.

The RFI team remains silent as they watch Mathis Reynolds approach Granger Mitchell with outstretched hand and after a few words place a tender kiss on Faye Mitchell's cheek. The greeting pauses when Malcolm and Gretchen approach them. Mathis excuses himself after introductions and heads inside the Church.

Funeral Service
Stacy Danielle Remington

Granger, Faye, Gretchen, and Malcolm are escorted to the front row of the stunningly beautiful house of worship. Gretchen whispers to the usher, "Perhaps there's a mistake, this row is most certainly for family." The usher smiles warmly at Gretchen, "No mistake, Ms. Mitchell."

The RFI team is escorted to the row behind the Mitchells, et al. Manuel nudges Fred with his knee and head motions to the front row on the opposite side, where Mathis Reynolds is seated at the aisle, holding hands with an elderly woman who favors Stacy. "Grandmother?" Manuel whispers.

"Stacy was right, you're a damned good detective," Fred laughs.

After a few words from the clergy, and hymns from an award-winning choir, Mathis Reynolds stands, places a kiss atop the elderly woman's head, steps into the aisle, climbs a handful of stairs, and prepares to deliver the eulogy. He opens with a stunner. "Assembled here, in this magnificent house of worship, are some of the world's top investigators, agents and spies." He smiles and gives a tiny shake of his head. "I doubt there's a single one among you who figured out that I was not only Stacy's friend and lawyer, but I am also her husband, and I have been for many years."

Gasps lead to murmurings, that lead to giggles, that leads to laughter, that leads to clapping.

When the congregation quiets Mathis begins again, "Before some of you start wondering if you've said anything disparaging to either of us about the other of us, rest assured, we did not discuss such matters. Our relationship was personal—it had to be that way. Stacy was a crime-buster, and I am a defense attorney. Stacy and I are—were—on opposite sides of things in the professional arena, but we were very much on the same side when it came to protecting our privacy and our marriage. There are two very distinguished guests here today who know this to be true because they were the only people who attended our wedding. Granger and Faye Mitchell honored us as witnesses to the happiest day of our lives. Granger not only stood in as my best man, but he walked my bride down a tiny aisle, and presented me her hand in marriage."

Gretchen and Faye reach for Granger's hands, he squeezes both and holds tight.

Mathis pulls a steadying breath before continuing. “A young, tenacious, and some might say brazen, Stacy Remington, met Granger Mitchell when she was twelve years old. The distinguished, accomplished attorney was at Stacy’s school to deliver an inspirational speech about getting an education, charting a course, setting goals, and being ready for whatever life had in store. Stacy decided then and there that she was ready for life and approached Attorney Granger Mitchell. In the beat of a heart, he became her mentor, her friend, and her father-figure.” Mathis turns to address the humbled man in the front row, the one reserved for family, “Stacy loved you Granger—beyond all measure.”

Gretchen squeezes her father’s hand and aches for him as his head lowers and his tears begin to fall. For Granger, the room fades away…

He stopped his forward momentum when he felt a tug on his sleeve.

“I want to be you when I grow up.”

The larger-than-life-man reached into his breast pocket, pulled out his business card, handed it to the young girl and said, “Write me a letter about yourself. I will write back.”

No one there that day thought either one would write those letters—except for Stacy and Granger, that is. She wrote hers, and he wrote his, and then they wrote dozens more over the years—Stacy listing her accomplishments and her struggles, Granger mentoring and encouraging her when she questioned whether she'd ever really get out of Harlem.

"You get the grades, the rest will take care of itself," he said during a birthday phone call one year. The celebratory call was from Stacy to Granger, and it brought him such joy.

Stacy Remington got the grades and was accepted to every undergraduate college and university to which she applied. She chose the College of William & Mary for her undergraduate work…

"Why William & Mary," Granger asked the beaming high school graduate.

"It is one of the original nine Colonial colleges, and it would have beaten Harvard as the first chartered school of higher education in America had it not been for the 'Indian uprising' of 1622. I figure the first Remington to leave Harlem for advanced learning ought to do that learning at a historical place as fine as Williamsburg." She leaned in and whispered into Granger's ear, "Besides, if William & Mary was good enough for Presidents Thomas Jefferson, James Monroe, and John Tyler, it is good enough for Stacy Remington."

Granger laughed big at his spunky little friend and added, "Don't forget George Washington, he got his…"

"Surveyor's license from W&M," Stacy finished her mentor's sentence. "You ain't telling me something I don't already know, Mr. Granger."

He laughed again, "No, I suppose I'm not, Miss Stacy."

Manuel and Fred give Mathis a few minutes before stepping into the hour-long receiving line. "We'd like to head to DC sometime today, if that's acceptable, Mr. Reynolds."

"It's Mathis, please. I think it's prudent. My announcement may bring about a few discussions with the brass at the Bureau, so I'd like to at least try to honor Stacy's request. We have side by side townhouses, so you'll see me quite often during your stay. Our lives were a bit unconventional—our living arrangements even more so. There is a hidden doorway in each of our pantries that allows internal access between our places. I know it seems all cloak and dagger, but we wanted privacy for our relationship, and I wanted Stacy to have an escape from her premises, if she needed one. Rather than building her a panic room, I bought her an adjoining panic house," he offers a smile and a shake of his head. "My side is always unlocked. If you need anything just knock or come on in. And Detectives, you and your team are welcome to stay at Stacy's place for as long as you'd like."

The RFI team gathers together and makes plans. It's decided that Manuel and Leavy will drive directly to DC and stay at Stacy's. Fred will head back to The Compound to spend time with Kitt and Joseph, then he'll head to Stacy's the next day. Goodbyes are made and the team members head in their respective directions.

On the flight back to Nova Scotia, Rocco makes an announcement. "FBI Director Shelby Webber has appointed John Maxwell as interim FICA Director. When the RFI jet returns to DC tomorrow it will have Fred Serpico and John Maxwell on it. Additionally, RFI will be working with the FBI on The Realm and Tango investigation, as well as the murder investigations of Abigail Forrester, Celia Brettenvue, and Dominique Brettenvue. The Stacy Remington debacle is **our** case. Director Webber and I had a lengthy discussion about RFI's previous dismissal from certain cases. She provided an explanation that was most enlightening. John will be informed of this by the director. His position at FICA is intended to be a bridge between the FBI and RFI, and his departure necessitates his replacement. Leavy and Manuel have suggested the hipster kid who works for Malcolm Price as the ideal candidate."

Fred nods his agreement and offers a caution, "Rocco, Malcolm Price may not take kindly to us poaching Researcher Randy."

"Si, Mayor Price thanked me for talking with him before talking with The Kid. Malcolm is in support of this opportunity." Rocco finishes with an offer for John to say a few words.

The man who uses words sparingly simply says, "I'm good, thanks."

Selling real estate.
Mending fences.

Granger and Faye fly from New York to Lewisburg with Mr. and Mrs. Mayor. They wait through one of Gretchen's word-mashes about boa-constricting pregnancy wear, and for all to share a meal, before Granger broaches a tender subject.

"Gretchen, I am going to displease you greatly in the next few minutes. Please tread carefully as I am not myself. I expect my emotional state is going to be your argument of dissent, so I give you fair warning, don't use it."

Gretchen preempts her father, "You want to sell the Cottage and the Carriage House, don't you?"

"Very astute of you. Yes, that is the decision I have made."

Gretchen remains silent—for far too long.

"Are you employing the silent treatment?" her father inquires.

"No. No. I'm experiencing a bit of trouble hoisting my ass up to the high road is all. Do you have a timeframe in mind?"

"For your ass-hoisting?" He tries a smile.

"For the sale of the estate." She tries a smile.

"I've spoken with Sotheby's and they suggest I put the estate on the market in early spring. You will have plenty of time to spend there if you so choose. As for the contents of both places, you should go through and select whatever you'd like. Otherwise, Sotheby's will be handling the sale of certain pieces and the donation of others."

Granger gets up and walks to his daughter. He takes her hands into his and tears, "I love you, Gretchen. I appreciate your making this decision bearable for me. I know it is a blow to you, one I did not want to inflict, but I just cannot step foot on Old Estate Road again." He kisses his daughter's cheek, takes hold of his wife's hand, and heads to the privacy elevator.

Gretchen holds her tears then loses them all when she hears the tiny ping, signaling the end of an era.

In that moment, Malcolm packs away his remaining issues with Gretchen and approaches her. He presses himself full against her back and wraps his long arms around his woman and baby. "I'm sorry," he whispers against her cheek.

Gretchen turns and presses into her man, "I am the one who is sorry, Malcolm. Not about the estate, although that is a bitter pill, but I am so sorry for hurting you. You're my man, and I haven't honored the parts of you I love most. I love that you protect me and push against forces that might cause me pain. I love that you want to bring a child into this world with me. Malcolm, I promise I will never leave you or put any distance between us again—that is, if you still want me."

Malcolm kisses the top of Gretchen's head, "Just like I said on our wedding day, Forever, Woman."

Finding their way back.

David Cluster approaches Minty's Shack with a shout out, "Hey, Steve, it's Cluster, you still in there?"

The back door comes flying open, missing Cluster by inches, "What do you want?"

"An explanation."

Steve scoffs, "I owe explanations to more people than I can count, but you aren't one of them."

"I'm here on behalf of your wife and your kids. You most definitely owe them an explanation."

"Get the fuck off my property."

"Or what? You'll call the cops? I am the fucking cops, and you're the sorry asshole who's staying away from his wife and kids. Whatever you're doing here, or whatever you think you're doing here, you can do with your woman. Maura has what it takes to handle this with you. The question is, do you have the balls to handle it with her?"

A crack appears, so Cluster leans into it.

"You've been here for days, man. Are you working through your shit or just hiding from it?"

"It's my fault Stacy is dead, Cluster. How the fuck do I work through that?"

"Listen, man, I've been in the trees, on the rooftops, and in the holes, so I know what it takes to get a clean shot. I'm not minimizing here, but the bottom line is this, you didn't devise the plan, you didn't put Stacy in that room, you didn't control her movements, and you sure the hell didn't kill her."

The crack widens, so Cluster marches through it.

"Go home, Steve, before your marriage is the next casualty."

The crack is a canyon, so Cluster pulls his broken friend through it, holds him tight and rolls with his pain.

Steve spends some time on his deck and moving about his land while Cluster packs up, picks up, and closes up Minty's Shack. After a bit, he calls out to Steve, "Come on, Phelps, I'll drop you at the airport. It's time for you to go home—wherever the hell that is."

The Compound

Fred and Kitt have spent hours in each other's arms. He hasn't said his piece about the plan, the shooting, the fuckup, the weight he carries, or the loss he feels. He just holds his lifeline.

Kitt knows her man is working the past few days through in his own way. When he gets to where he needs to be, they'll be right again.

"Kittridge."

"Mmmmm."

"You know I want you in every way, but tonight I need you. I need to take you." Fred pulls her out straight and begins his journey into her. She is already where she needs to be to accept him. Fred groans as he finds and hits all the right spots. His woman's sex sounds are familiar, her movements and hunger begin claiming him. Fred doesn't hold back. He is urgent, selfish. He needs release, in his head, in his heart, in his woman. He takes what he needs, and leaves himself deep. He rolls from her, pulls her to him, rides his pain, then leaves it behind. They stay in one another's embrace, and when the new day breaks, so too does the turbulence in Fred.

"Kittridge."

"Yes."

"I'm happy."

"Me, too."

Rocco Fiancetti pulls the RFI Land Rover as close to the tarmac as possible. Fred and John hop out and head to the back for their gear. A voice from an approaching man calls from over their shoulder, "You think I could hitch a ride to The Compound."

The men wait for Steve, he goes directly to Fred, "Fuck you, too."

Fred smiles so wide his cheeks suffer the pain. He pulls his best friend close, "It's damn good to see you, Steve. Unfortunately, I'm heading out of town for a few."

"Don't care where the fuck you're going. I'm here to see if my woman still wants me."

"Spoiler alert, she wants the hell out of you," Fred says with a slap to Steve's shoulder.

The guys update their returning team member on what's happened during the past week. He bristles when he hears that John has been named as Stacy's interim replacement, then smacks John on the back with a, "Good luck in the snake pit."

Rocco and Steve wait until the RFI jet is wheels up before heading home. It is many minutes before Rocco speaks, "Have your contemplations been fruitful?"

"Not sure." Steve leans his seat back, closes his eyes, and contemplates .... fruitfully…

Mike and Steve canvassed the area behind the Cottage and Carriage House when they first arrived looking for the assassin's fire sight.

"Steve, the killer made his approach to the Celia Brettenvue murder scene through those woods. It's a three-quarter mile trail that he's set with reflective tape markers. There's no way he trekked through and went directly into the Carriage House for the killing. He had to have set a surveillance spot somewhere in this area," Mike suggested.

"Like this one?" Steve smiled and pointed.

"Yeah, like that one."

The men surveilled the lair without disturbing it. “From this vantage point, he has a perfect view of the back door. And inside the kitchen of the Cottage, and he has a perfect view into the Carriage House. Fred and Manuel will need to stay low while they wait.” Steve scanned the surrounding area, looking for the right place to lie in wait for his target. “There. That tree’s perfect.” He scanned again and pointed to an area 500 yards in the opposite direction from the killer’s lair, “You should set up there. There’s a small retaining wall along where the land slopes down. You’ll be plenty obscured in the gully. Ferraro might not expect company in the woods, but he’s trained military, he’ll be looking. That spot will keep you out of sight.”

“He’ll have night vision.”

“Taking chances here, Mike. Our goal is to ‘lure and capture’. We should be prepared to shoot to kill.”

The planning and readying behind them, the RFI shooters got in place and set for action. The backup RFI shooter updated his team, “200 yards from lair.” He and Steve trained their scopes on the assassin as he settled in, set his tripod, and secured his rifle.

Steve whispered, “He’s mounted.”

Boston took his binoculars and scanned the bottom floor of the Cottage, then the upstairs, then the bottom floor again. He lowered his hand a fraction of an inch, turned his head slightly to the left toward Steve, raised the viewers again, and scanned the woods; first in

Mike's direction, then toward the Carriage House, then back to the Cottage. He put the binoculars aside, checked the time on his watch, went flat on his stomach, inched into place, sighted through his scope, and waited for the visual on his victim.

Mike and Steve went on high alert when they heard Stacy Remington greet Granger Mitchell from inside the Cottage. All three men in the tree line got ready when Stacy Remington and Granger Mitchell entered the kitchen.

Boston sighted, moved his finger to the trigger…

"He's ready for shot…"

The assassin lifted his head a fraction, turned left—And. Pulled. The. Trigger.

"Granger and Stacy down!" Mike yelled.

Steve shot his target and yelled, "**Shooter down. MOVE. MOVE. MOVE!"**

Steve startles the fuck awake. "Something's wrong. Something's fucking wrong with that shit."

Rocco offers his opinion, "Si."

Staying here beats all.

Manuel wakes to find Leavy in the kitchen of Stacy Remington's townhouse frying bacon, scrambling eggs, and perking coffee, "Woman, you do this?"

"I like to eat; cooking begets eating. Pull up a seat." Leavy pours Manuel an enormous mug of black coffee and brings it to him. "You slept like shit. Drink up, we've got a lot of work to do. Fred will be here soon."

When she tries to hand off a plate of food, she realizes she's lost Manuel's attention, "You're truly stupefied by the photos of Stacy and Mathis."

He grunts into his coffee. "Aren't you? There's a damned love story in those pictures, Leavy."

"They were married for years, Manuel, what did you expect?"

"I don't know, but I didn't expect Mr. and Mrs. Whitewater Rafting, or Mr. and Mrs. Hot Air Ballooning, or Mr. and Mrs. Sand and Surf-sexing for fuck's sake. I've known Director Remington for five years and I've never seen her so much as crack the edges of a smile."

Leavy places the plate of food on the table, "Eat, you're becoming hysterical." The chuckling woman leaves to answer a knock on the front door.

Manuel points, "The knock is coming from the pantry."

"Staying here beats all," she giggles as she answers the pantry door. "Mathis, did we bother you?"

"No, not at all, the smell of food beckoned me."

"Sit, there's plenty. How do you take your coffee?"

"Black usually, today I'd prefer it intravenously, if possible."

Leavy hands him a huge mug, gently touches his shoulder, and goes about setting another pot. She talks over her shoulder, "Manuel's having a little trouble reconciling his former boss with the woman in your amazing pictures." She laughs at the growl that comes from her man.

Mathis nods over his cup of Joe, "My wife was nothing like the woman you worked with, Manuel. She was outrageously funny, completely unguarded emotionally, and when she loved, she loved deeply."

Manuel drops his fork onto his plate, "Due respect, but are you busting my balls, and if you are not, how did I not see any of that, sir?"

Mathis laughs, "I find this rather amusing, Manuel, given that you are the son of Rocco Fiancetti. Stacy said the MI6 Operative is British through and through, yet feigns a kitschy Italian persona and language. His people ignore the truth of who he is and readily accept what he portrays." Mathis pulls a few sips. "I guess there's a lesson here."

"And that is?"

"No one is as they seem to be on the surface."

Manuel shakes his head in an effort to wrap it around the woman he wished he'd known.

"With no harm intended, Manuel, my wife is dead because we all ignored the truth—Stacy could never be with Granger Mitchell at a moment of peril and not do everything possible to protect him."

The men sit in silence, share a meal, and their private thoughts of Stacy. On his way back through the pantry Mathis grabs a couple cans of soup.

Leavy squeals, "Staying here beats all."

Fred arrives at the townhouse shortly after Mathis heads through the pantry wall. He and Manuel leave Leavy to her jovial comments about wall-walkers and head upstairs to Stacy's office. They are p.u.s.h.e.d. b.a c.k. by the tomblike feel.

"God, Fred, it's only been a few days, and it feels like this place knows she gone. It's eerie."

Fred starts doing his thing at a window overlooking a postage-stamp-size front yard. He has just started pulling at a mental thread when he notices a car inch by the townhouse—the driver clearly looking at the place.

"Black Lexus."

Manuel stops reviewing a file, "What?"

"A black Lexus just did a creep past the townhouse."

Manuel hands a file to Fred, "This has your name on it. It's pretty thick."

The detective opens it while still standing at the window. He flips through a few pages, "It's the Leavy kidnapping file."

Manuel stops what he's doing, "What kidnapping file?"

"When Leavy was missing, I continued my own search for her, even though I'd been removed from the case. At that time, no one knew you had rescued her and John Maxwell had hidden her, so I kept looking for the kidnapped FICA agent. I sent copies of my case files to Stacy for safe keeping." He flips through the notes and begins nodding at the familiar documents within. "Not sure you know, but I spent some time at the Carriage House going over Granger's notes, the ones where he documented his meetings with the Brettenvue women. There was an entry that referenced the kidnapping of FICA Agent Hannah Leavy. Apparently, Dominique told Granger the kidnapping was significant beyond the kidnapping itself. The notes failed to include the essential component as to why it was significant. I made a mental note to review my file on Leavy's kidnapping. Now, here I am holding a copy of that file." Fred turns back to the window to process.

"Black Lexus," he says for the second time in a handful of minutes.

Leavy enters the home office, "What about a black Lexus?"

"It's been passing the townhouse," Fred informs her.

Leavy takes a stroll around the home office. "With all this equipment, Stacy probably has outside security cameras. Manuel, where's the security access codes for Stacy's—"

Before Leavy finishes her question, Fred body slams her to the floor, lays on top of her to shield her from shards of flying glass that burst into the room.

"Shooter!" Fred yells to Manuel, who is already crawling to Leavy. He pulls her from beneath his partner and out into the hall. Fred scrambles to the window knowing full well that the Lexus is long gone. He runs to the hallway where Manuel is tending to a cut on Leavy's arm, "She's out cold. Check the bathroom for gauze and shit to clean and close this cut. See if you can find smelling salts," Manuel directs.

"Not the bathroom—" Mathis interrupts, then stops, when Fred and Manuel train their guns on him. "Jesus, put those away. I heard the ruckus and came to help. Damn white cops pulling guns on black men, it's epidemic I tell you," Mathis lectures as he makes his way to a linen closet not far from where Leavy and the men are. He hands a medical kit to Manuel, "How long has she been out?"

"A minute or so."

"She needs to be seen; I'll call for an ambulance."

Again, Mathis stops cold when Fred and Manuel yell, "No!"

"If you call this in, the cops will come, they'll search this place and find FBI files all over Stacy's office. They'll kick us out, take what they want, and let the Feds take the rest. We'll lose custody of what's in that room," Fred explains. "We need to get rid of the gunshot evidence before someone on the street calls it in," Fred suggests.

Mathis walks around the medical scene, "Stay out of Stacy's office. I have a plan."

Minutes later a baseball comes flying through the already broken window, the ball rolls into the hallway stopping inches from Leavy. Fred peers into the office and starts laughing just as Mathis gets back upstairs.

"Nice move. If the cops come all they'll find is a busted-up window from a baseball." Fred stops talking when he hears Manuel.

"Welcome back, Leavy," he says as she opens her eyes.

She moans and touches the back of her head. "What happened?" She eyes the men, then the baseball on the floor beside her, "Did I get hit with a baseball? No wonder my head hurts."

Mathis smiles warmly at the woozy woman, "Do you want to get up or stay there until the doctor comes?"

"What doctor?" Manuel and Fred say in unison.

"Eli Reynolds, my brother. I called him after I tossed the ball."

"You threw the ball at me?" Leavy asks, clearly confused.

"Of course not. I threw it after you were unconscious."

"You played baseball **after** I got injured?"

"Well, I…" Mathis paused, "some things can't be explained adequately, Leavy. Just know that I had a good reason."

Fred laughs, "Nice throw, by the way."

Mathis hit me with a baseball.

Manuel and Fred help Leavy to a sitting position, as Mathis runs to let Eli in. The RFI men recognize Dr. Eli Reynolds as an attendee at Stacy's funeral. Both are struck by the stark contrast between the brothers. Mathis is just under six feet tall, wears his black hair cropped, his impeccably tailored suits well, and his wingtips spit-polish shiny. Eli is a few inches over six feet, wears his black hair dreaded and banded, and his earthy-crunchy clothes comfortably worn.

The doctor crouches next to his patient. "Hi Leavy, I'm Eli. I hear you've taken a hit to your head. Can you tell me how it happened?"

"Mathis hit me with a baseball," she's wearing a face full of 'I can't explain it' confusion.

Eli sees the baseball on the floor and raises a questioning eye toward his brother.

"Of course, I did not hit her with the baseball, Eli. Fred tackled her to the floor to avoid a bullet."

"Oh, well then, that makes this so much better. Were you present during the shooting, brother? Because if so, you'd be well advised to tell these two that white men with guns and men with black skin do not generally mix well?"

“He told us,” Fred and Manuel say in unison and on a shared laugh.

Dr. Eli Reynolds abandons talking for examining. After several minutes, he makes his diagnosis, “The patient exhibits a delay in her response to questions, and has event amnesia to a certain degree, as well as a headache she grades as a 4 on a scale of 10. She has dizziness, intermittent nausea, her vision and hearing are fine, and by the end of the neurological exam her balance, coordination and reflexes are no better or worse than they were when the exam began." Eli approves the decision to keep Leavy at Stacy’s provided she is observed continuously for 48-hours and taken to the hospital if any of her symptoms worsen or new issues present themselves. He prescribes bed rest, that she be woken every 2-4 hours for evaluation of rousing, and acetaminophen for her headaches.

Once the concussive injury is taken care of, Eli goes about cleaning and stitching the cut on her forearm. “Keep the wound and bandages dry, change the dressing twice a day, and use this antibiotic ointment. Manuel, you clearly have triage experience, so you can remove the stitches in 7-10 days, or I can come back. Fred and Mathis, let’s talk elsewhere.”

Eli leads the men closer to Stacy’s office, “Mathis, explain.”

"Stacy's houseguests are members of Rocco Fiancetti Incorporated. She left them information in her office on a case they are all working. They are here in that capacity, but also as houseguests. Apparently, Detective Serpico noticed a black Lexus driving by the townhouse. On the last trip past, the driver shot out that window," Mathis points, "Fred tackled Leavy, kept her from a bullet, but knocked her out cold."

Eli steps into the room for a better view. "Too much damage for a bullet." He turns to his brother, "Did you throw a baseball to further the damage?"

Mathis nods, "The men didn't want evidence of a shooting in case the cops came by," Mathis shrugs his shoulders.

"Hmmm, two white men didn't want the cops to come to a shooting at a black man's house—that's something new," Eli says with a cocky smile.

Fred laughs, "You do know you are in the presence of two armed white cops, right?"

"I know and I'm experiencing a certain amount of sweat in concealed areas," Eli shares Fred's laugh.

"No worries, Eli. I flunked the Ishihara test."

The doctor chuckles, "You're color blind?"

Fred laughs, "Only when it comes to the color black."

The black man enjoys the banter with the white cop. He tilts his head back, "I like you Fred."

Fred nods, then changes the subject, "That was one hell of a pitch, Attorney Reynolds."

Eli jumps in, "Fred, you happen to be in the presence of Marksman Mathis, best damned NCAA Division I ball thrower of his day. I've seen this man hit a nickel taped to the side of a barn from ninety feet."

Fred smiles and shrugs.

"Not impressed, Detective? You will be. The Marksman hit the penny while blindfolded."

Fred smiles wide, "No shit?"

"I shit you not, my friend," the sibling says with the pride that only a younger brother can feel.

Mathis shakes his head, "I think we've had enough about my glory days, little brother. Eli if you aren't busy come back at six, we've having pizza and beers."

Eli accepts.

Fred slaps Mathis on the shoulder as he steps full into Stacy's room, "I better get to work on this mess, then. See you later Eli, and to be on the safe side when you approach the door tonight, have your hands on your head and your feet spread."

Eli and Mathis crack up.

Eli winks. Manuel growls.
Leavy laughs.

Felicity Ferraro, Realm operative and handler of its assassin's team takes a call. "Is it done?" she asks with an edge to her voice.

"The shot was taken without casualties as you requested. I waited until Fred Serpico saw the Lexus come to a stop, the lowering of the window, and the inching of the gun out that window. He hit the ground just before I fired. That's the good news. The bad news is that DC cops aren't on scene because RFI didn't call it in."

"Why not?"

"RFI knows if the cops get into the townhouse and mess around in Remington's office, it will be sealed, and the RFI team won't be able to continue their work. They're good, Felicity, this isn't going to be a cake walk with them."

"You're a cop. Go to the door, say you're responding to a noise complaint, I don't care, just get inside," she demands.

"I'm not a cop. I'm a high-ranking, gold-badge wearing, assistant chief of Investigative Services for the DC Metropolitan Police Department. I don't show up at fucking noise complaints. Besides, Mathis Reynolds lives next door, he'd lawyer the fuck out of any cop trying to get inside Remington's townhouse. You do know that Mathis came out at the funeral as Remington's husband?"

"I heard. Why does he live next door?"

"They kept their marriage secret for some reason. Side by side townhouses helped the subterfuge I guess. So, now what?"

"I want Remington's files and whatever she has on her computers. And I want whatever is at the Mitchell Carriage House in Philly. Those are the files that Boston was after the night he fucked up," she hisses.

"Let me work on those, then."

"Fine. Mason, no fuck ups," she warns.

Remington Townhouse

Fred cleans Stacy's office of broken glass and a small blood stain on the carpet. While he cleans things, the stuff he read in Dominique's files starts a loop in his head and a churn in his gut, "I left the Brettenvue women's files at the Carriage House before returning Janelle's Jeep to Ted." The looping and churning prompts a phone call.

"Hey, Granger, it's Fred."

"Still have caller ID, but I appreciate your announcement, Fred."

"I'm beginning to see where Gretchen gets her pithiness."

"Yeah, she's a pisser. So, what can I do for you?"

"I want to send Philly Detective, Ted Brothers, to the Carriage House to get the Brettenvue files. He still has a set of keys, and if you haven't changed the security code, he is good to go."

"I'll call the guard shack and inform them about Detective Brothers' visit and tell them that you'll notify them directly the next time you want access to my property."

"That works, but you do know this means we won't be talking much?"

Granger chuckles, "There are prices to pay in life, Fred. I guess hearing from you infrequently is the price I get to pay."

"Pisser."

"Call anytime, Fred."

"You, too, Granger."

Fred immediately calls Ted, "How's Penny?" he asks without so much as a greeting.

"Antsy, feisty, sexy as fuck," Ted groans.

"She about ready for some tension breaking?" Fred laughs.

"Just about. As for me, I'm beyond ready for that woman."

"Maybe you two want to go for a ride tonight? Shit, let me rephrase that. Can you two head over to the Mitchell Carriage House and get the Dominique and Celia files and hold onto them until further notice? Your visit is approved by Granger and the guard shack knows you'll be coming."

"Will do. This will be good for Lucky; she needs to get out."

Fred chuckles, "You call her Lucky? Best damn nickname ever, given she lived through one of Boston's assassination attempts. Tell her hello for me and I'll be in touch. Thanks, Ted."

Fred heads to Stacy's bedroom to check on Leavy and update Manuel. He finds them asleep.

Mathis answers his brother's knock at Stacy's townhouse door at precisely 6 PM. Eli spins into the room, pushes his chest against the wall, puts his hands onto the top of his head, and spreads his legs.

Fred cracks up, "Gonna be tough eating pizza and guzzling beer in that pose, but if you're planning to stay that way your feet are too close, so spread them wider."

Eli pushes off the wall and saunters into the living room. He finds Leavy nestled onto the couch, "Resting comfortably, I see." He walks to her, looks into her eyes for an unnecessarily l.o.n.g. time.

"Is something wrong?" Leavy asks.

"Nope. I just got lost in your eyes, they're beautiful," Eli winks.

Manuel growls.

Leavy laughs, then says, "Ouch," and touches her head.

"Too soon?" Eli asks.

"A bit."

The detective and the doctor head to the kitchen to grab pizzas and a cooler of beers and sodas.

"You know, Fred, it's good that you guys are here. Mathis is introspective by nature and left on his own he'd be a brooding mess by now. I wouldn't be at all surprised if Stacy wanted you here for that very reason. That woman loved that man in ways I've never seen and have never experienced."

Fred shakes his head a bit, "Manuel is freaked out at the differences between FICA Director Remington and Mrs. Mathis Reynolds. Truth be told, I'm caught off the rails on it, too."

"Stacy gave nothing of her true self to anyone but Mathis and Granger. I benefited in knowing Stacy because of proximity, and she was genuinely lovely to me, but there were two distinct sides to Stacy, and never the twain did meet."

Pizza, beers, stories, and laughs fill the corners of Stacy's townhouse that night. At one point Leavy nestles down and drifts off. The men move their merriment to the kitchen, where before long Mathis broaches the last case Stacy worked.

"I was concerned and very surprised that Stacy kept working a case Director Webber removed her from. Disobeying a directive was very unlike Stacy."

Manuel nods, "I only knew the director as being by the books, but she was onto something when she was pulled."

Fred starts to say something, pulls short.

"Something wrong?" Eli asks.

"Something nagging," He drains his beer and accepts another from Manuel. "Stacy left a file for me upstairs. I was flipping through it when the window busted out."

"Yeah, right, you said the file was about Leavy."

"About her kidnapping." Since the kidnapping and rescue of Agent Hannah Leavy had not been well-publicized, Fred explains a bit for the Reynolds brothers. "Director Remington originally put me and my partner, Steve Phelps, on the case. We were with Leavy when she was taken and worked our asses off pulling the tiniest threads to get a lead on her. Then, out of the blue, Stacy called and fired us. A week or so later, Stacy asked if I'd continue the search on my own—which I'd already been doing, anyway. I sent her copies of my case files—that's the stuff in the file Stacy left for me upstairs." Fred pulls a sip of beer. "I'd just started flipping through the file titled, Peru, when a black Lexus that'd driven past the townhouse a couple of times stopped. The driver lowered the window and took a shot."

"What does Peru have to do with Leavy?" Eli asks.

"She was kidnapped by Realm associates, taken to a warehouse in Chelsea, and prepared for shipment on an LNG tanker with a final destination of Peru."

"We should focus our investigation on LNG," Leavy says from behind the men causing two of them to jump from the table.

Manuel and Eli move to her, "You shouldn't be up," they say in unison.

"Sorry, boys, but I need to pee. Since the fine doctor didn't catheter me, I see no other option than to ambulate myself to the bathroom."

"The woman is using medical terminology, that's so hot."

Eli swoons.

Manuel growls.

Leavy laughs, "Ouch," she says as her hand finds its way to the bump on the back of her head.

Fred is waiting for her in the kitchen, the others had moved back to the living room. Leavy smiles, "Are you my escort?" Fred offers her his arm, "LNG. You were about to tell me about LNG."

"I was?"

The men wait for Leavy to get comfortable, then shoot a questioning look at Eli, "Let her settle. She's hunting right now, it's part of her brain injury which is after all what a concussion is. Let her work the question through for herself. Whatever it was that she wanted to say will either come again, or it won't. Let's wait and see how much she remembers."

It takes a while, but it comes again. Her words are slow, but the story is there. "Joy, Annie, and I were working The Realm case when the three of us were in protective custody at The Compound."

Eli turns skeptical eyes, suddenly unsure of his patient's mental capacity.

"She's coherent," Fred says.

"Kidnappings, protective custody, compounds, what the fuck goes on in this world?" Eli asks softly.

Leavy smiles and continues. "Joy had these white boards all over the Computer Center. One of the boards was dedicated to identifying The Realm leaders—this was before Dominique named them during the interrogation after her failed coup attempt. We had a few leaders identified, maybe three or four. I think those leaders were from South America, one of them was the Peruvian crime-lord, Antonio .... Alvarez. He was the one who ordered my kidnapping, had me put into a steel drum, and arranged for me to be shipped on an LNG tanker."

Eli shakes his head, "Coup attempt. Women being shipped in drums on tankers."

"The other leaders, the ones who we thought were leaders, were from countries that had LNG exports or imports or something. I can't really remember the specifics, but I know our work ended when Dominique rolled on everyone. At that time, RFI hadn't heard the word Tango, so we thought we'd put the nefarious organization out of commission. Manuel, you should call Joy; she doesn't have a concussion and might remember more."

Eli stands and goes to Leavy, "Okay, that's enough. You need to be taken to bed," he smirks at Manuel. "Would you like the honors, or should I?"

Eli laughs.

Manuel growls.

Leavy laughs. "Ouch."

Reporting in.

"There is a problem with RFI," the surveillance manager reports in.

"Details?"

"They've worked a few things through. They know Tango is a program involving LNG and that the thugs behind bars aren't the leaders of The Realm."

"Have they made a connection to anyone in the Gang of Eight?"

"If they have, they haven't said anything about it while at Remington's townhouse or in her car."

"Her car?"

"Serpico has been using it."

"What's the immediate concern?"

"All of it. The longer they stay at Remington's, the greater the chance they'll find something. I was hoping Remington's surprise husband, Mathis Reynolds, would tire of them being around, but he and his brother are enjoying the company."

"Keep them under surveillance."

Turner Rodgers, the supposed leader of The Realm calls his boss, "Did you get all that?"

"Every word. Jack Johnson's assessment is correct. It's time for RFI to move out of

Director Remington's townhouse. That means it is time for The Realm to get one of the cyber huntresses in their hands."

Do you want a two-for?

Researcher Randy answers a blocked number with his standard, "Yo."

"I, Rocco Fiancetti, request discussions with Researcher Randy."

"Discuss away, Fathering One of the Offspringing One."

Rocco laughs heartily, "You're hired. The RFI jet will be in Lewisburg tomorrow."

"I'll be aboard with my plus one," Randy says before disconnecting.

He pulls the Justice close, "Want to spend the rest of your Thanksgiving break at a spy compound?"

Peyton laughs, "I was just wondering what I'd do for the rest of November."

"I've a few suggestions." Randy flips his babe onto her back and proves his point.

Philly

The high-ranking, gold-badge wearing, assistant chief of Investigative Services for the DC Metropolitan Police Department watches from the tree line as a buff black dude enters and exits the Mitchell Carriage House. Gold Badge snaps a series of pictures as the guy hefts several boxes out to his ride. The interloper gets another set of pictures of a woman resting in the passenger seat of the Land Rover. The Realm associate starts trudging back through the trees, "Fucking Philly. Every fucking time we try to get our hands on those files, some dude fucks it up—the hipster kid at the law office, now the guy in the Land Rover." Gold Badge picks up his pace along the yellow tape trail in Granger's woods, hops into his Lexus, plugs the black dude's picture into a facial recognition program and waits. "Detective Theodore Brothers, Philadelphia PD, let's see what else there is to find out about you." He pulls up another program and begins his research, "Drexel Hill residency, you've been on the force a decade, moved up through the ranks, are a respected member of the force, lost your wife in the Track Mall Massacre."

Gold Badge repeats the process on the woman. "Army Reservist Penelope Meehan. I don't need to put you through any other program, you're the reporter Boston almost took out. 'Almost' being the operative and unacceptable word." He closes his laptop. "Last I heard, you were pretty fucked up, Ms. Meehan. If you're out on a joy ride with the detective, and your place of residence is Lewisburg, 1+1 says you're probably staying at his place."

Trellis places a call to his handler, "Irish, I just left the Carriage House. PPD Detective Ted Brothers beat me to the punch. He took several boxes out an hour or so ago; they're probably the files we want. The detective's tagalong on the ride from Drexel was the reporter your husband failed to eliminate. Do you want a two-for tonight?"

"Yes."

Drexel Hill

Ted wakes Penny when he pulls into the attached garage and leads her through a covered breezeway to the house. The ride to and fro wiped her out, but she's slept and is now getting her second wind. She touches Ted's cheek, "Can you give me a few minutes?"

"Sure. Holler if you need me."

So far, she hasn't hollered.

From behind closed bathroom door, the sound of Penny's call puts Ted into motion. He rushes to bathroom and bangs, "Lucky. Are you okay?"

"I could use some help, actually."

Ted eases the door open, not sure what to expect—for the record, he does not expect what he finds. Penny is standing in the center of the room, barely wearing a beautiful coral peek-through robe, tied loosely around her waist and ending mid-thigh.

"Ted, I can't wait another second for you to touch me. I'm not sure what we can do, but I need to be near you."

Ted pulls his sweater over his head and moves to the woman he wants to claim as his own. He unties her robe and gently slides it over her shoulders. He sees that she has wrapped her bandages in plastic signaling a shower is in store for them. Ted slowly takes in the breathtaking form of Penny. He palms her cheek then traces his thumb across her lip, down her neck and along the swell of her breasts. They immediately respond to his touch. His fingers find her nipples for a quick twirl then move down her sides and along the five-pointed Army star that is tattooed on the flat between her belly button and her mound. A groan settles in his throat. He kisses her tenderly, losing himself for a moment in the taste of her.

He steps away, his want pressing hard against his jeans. The man who wants this woman turns on the shower and undresses fully. Penny smiles and steps to him, takes him in her hand then presses her hips against him.

He steps away, "It's been a long time Penny, let me lead, or I won't last." They hold hands as they step into the oversized shower. He puts his back to the spray and leans her gently against the wall. He lathers her, slicks the length of her, and cups water in his hands to rinse her. His kisses and touches bring her quickly to panting arousal.

Ted shuts off the water and kneels onto the floor, his ass resting back on his legs. He positions Penny in front of him, "What do you think?"

She puts her feet on either side of his legs, "I think I want you—I need you in me."

He kisses and teases her as she begins to lower herself. He guides himself in and eases her hips down until she's taken the length of him. Her whimpers thrill the man who's wanted to be in her from the moment he laid eyes on her. Ted supports her back gently as he kisses, nibbles, and sucks. Penny rocks and nestles, raises and lowers the length of him. When her sexual joy hits, it is immediately met with his sexual claim.

The satisfied lovers hold one another through postcoital quivers and pulses. Ted lifts Penny's chin and exams her beautiful face, her eyes are hooded and still out of focus, "Hey, you look as though I might lose you. Let me help you up."

Penny wants to do it by herself, but she just can't. Ted gets her to her feet and out of the shower.

"An awkward ending to a great fuck," she laughs.

He towels her dry, then unwraps the plastic on her shoulder. He pulls a thick terry cloth bath towel around her and buffers her sway as they move through the kitchen to the den. Ted realizes he is losing her quickly. He lifts the spent woman and carries her to the couch, then rummages quickly through the bureau, finds a floor-length, button-down flannel nightgown.

"Can you get up, Penny?" He helps her up, wraps the nightgown around her back, puts her good arm through a long sleeve and leaves the other sleeve hanging down. When Penny is buttoned up, he takes the hanging sleeve and wraps it across her front and tucks it into a pocket on the side of the gown.

Penny eyes the couch, "How long before you're ready?"

"No couch, tonight, Lucky. It's back to the recliner for you."

"But, Ted, I love it when you hold me. I sleep more soundly."

Ted takes Penny's face into his hands, "I've been inside you, Lucky. I want to be there again. Trust me, you would not get a moment's rest if you were pressed against my wood all night."

She sways against him, "Help," is the last word she says before he places her onto her recliner and tucks her in tight.

Breezeways, bullets, boxes, and briefcases.

Penny startles awake. The feeling she had the night she was shot is back. She tries to push it down with reason, "The assassin is behind bars. The assassin is injured and can't shoot anyone." Fear bubbles through reason, "He tried to kill me, there is a reason why he tried to kill me…he didn't kill me, but the reason he wanted me dead is still there." Penny hears a faint scratching noise.

The Army Reservist springs into action, she lowers her recliner and moves next to Ted, puts her hand over his mouth, "Shhhhh, someone is breaking in."

Ted eases his chair down and takes his weapon off the end table. "Where?"

"Back door breezeway."

"Can you get upstairs?"

Penny nods.

"There's a Glock in the end table next to the bed, second door on the left. Call it in."

They move in different directions. Penny goes up the stairs. Ted goes out the front door. She is on the phone with dispatch when she hears Ted yell. "Police, freeze," the words are followed by two rapid fire gunshots. The Army Reservist is in full control. She tells dispatch there's an officer involved shooting—dispatch tells her to stay in place—she does not stay in place. She moves through the house and out the front door, eases along to its corner, pauses when footfalls head her way. "Ted."

"Hold your fire, Lucky, I'm heading your way. Whoever the fuck our visitor is, he's dead." Ted corners to find a frigid, shaking mess. He tries to take the Glock from Penny's hand

She wraps her fingers tight.

"Penny, give me the gun."

She gently shakes her head.

"Penny, it's over, I need your gun."

Penny's eyes focus on Ted's face, she loosens her grip.

Ted eases the gun free. "Come on, let's get you inside. How the hell did you even get out here?"

Ted makes quick work of tucking Penny onto her recliner and heads back outside to meet the arriving force. He grabs his cell and pushes a button.

Fred answers the call, "Just heading to bed, Theodore."

"There's been a shooting at my place. Whoever tried to get into my house is dead in my breezeway. I think he came to finish Boston's job. And Fred, I picked up the files a couple hours ago."

"Are you and Pen—" Fred's words are cut short.

"Ah, shit. Fred I've got to go, I might have caught the fucker's bullet."

Fred is in Philly in under two hours. Driving Stacy's government vehicle with bubble light and siren helped him accomplish that feat. He shows his credentials to three cops before being allowed into Ted's house. He exhales a huge sigh when he sees the Philly detective, sans shirt and sporting only a bicep medical wrap.

"Flesh wound?" Fred asks.

"Few stitches, but yeah," Ted smiles. He tosses a head shrug at an out-cold Penny, "She's an amazing woman. Come on let's get some coffee."

Ted sits down and talks, Fred sets coffee and listens.

"So, I woke up with Penny's hand over my mouth, she whispered, 'shhhhh, someone is breaking in, back door breezeway.' I sent her upstairs, told her where my Glock was, and told her to call it in. I headed out the front door, and when I rounded the corner I yelled, 'Police, freeze!' The guy spun, pointed his gun, and the two of us shot at each other like we were part of some fucking pop up arcade game. My bullet hit the guy. The guy hit the ground and wasn't moving, so I inched toward him and kicked his weapon free. I was checking his vitals when I heard Penny whisper my name. I told her I was approaching so she didn't shoot the fuck out of me, and when I got to her, she's standing with her back pressed against the corner of the house. She had the Glock in the only useable hand she has, and the cordless phone was tucked into the pocket of her nightgown with dispatch still on the line. She was barefoot and shivering and wobbling like a newborn filly. I talked the weapon out of her hand and got her onto the recliner where she passed out cold. She's been out cold ever since."

A fearful call comes from the den, "Ted."

"Shit. Penny doesn't know I was hit. You go while I put on a shirt," Ted instructs.

Fred steps into the den, "Hey, Penny. Ted will be right in. Can I get you anything?"

"What's wrong? Why are you talking like that? Is Ted hurt?"

"Geez, you can take the girl out of the newsroom, but you can't take the nosey out of the girl," Fred smiles.

Penny glowers.

Fred breaks. "Okay, okay, Ted has a flesh wound. F.L.E.S.H. wound. It's been stitched and wrapped. He went to get a shirt so you wouldn't freak. You're not going to freak, right?"

"Not if I see him within the next goddamn minute, Fred."

Ted comes into the room totally enjoying the push and pull of his friend and his woman, "I'm here, Lucky. You feeling okay?"

"Perhaps I should be asking you that question, Ted. Where did you get your F.L.E.S.H. wound?"

The injured detective shoots a "gee-thanks" look to his partner, then answers the worrying woman. "Bicep. Seven stiches and I'm good to go. And you haven't answered my question, you feeling okay?"

"I'm feeling like I need to pee and am in desperate need of some headache OTCs. So, if you two will give me an assist out of this chair, I'll be on my way."

Fred does the honors. He walks with her to the bathroom, "I have a couple questions if you're up to it."

"In the bathroom?" Penny asks astounded.

Fred laughs big, "I was hoping we could **both** sit, so I'll wait until you're back in the den."

Ted eyes the laughing Fred, "What's so funny?"

"Your woman. I think I might have a bit of a crush on her."

Ted snorts, "I'm way ahead of you, man. I'm falling hard for that woman."

Fred stays the night with Ted and Penny, and at first morning's light he is heading to the kitchen to put on coffee when he sidetracks to answer a knock on the front door. A young Philly PD officer standing there asks to speak with Detective Ted Brothers.

"What's up, Landry?" Ted asks as he nears the duo.

"I know you aren't on this case, Detective, being as you are one of the shooters from last night, but the perp's car is over on Laird. I was just there on a strange vehicle call when I saw DC license plates; thought you might want to take a swing by before I call it in."

"The perp is from DC?" Fred asks. "Any chance the car is a black Lexus?"

The officer looks at Ted before answering. He receives a nod. "Yes, sir, a black Lexus."

Fred shoots Ted a look that says 'there's more to this story.'

Ted puts a pin in it for a minute, "Landry, any ID on the perp?"

"You don't know, sir?"

Brothers shakes his head.

"Detective, the man you shot and killed last night is Mason Trellis, assistant chief of Investigative Services for the DC Metropolitan Police Department."

"What the fuck?" Ted and Fred unison.

DC

John Maxwell has been in Washington for days and has yet to lay eyes on his boss, Shelby Webber. The interim FICA director has spent those days—those very long days—pouring over his predecessor's files. With each file pulled and reviewed, he mutters the same thing, "Complete. Succinct. Analytical." John gets up from his desk, goes to an enormous white board, stares at it for several minutes, then titles it, THE REALM. He is just about to fill it with information and questions when a knock comes.

The director enters and approaches John Maxwell with outstretched hand, "I wanted to meet with you sooner, John," she palms him a slip of paper, "but there have been questions to answer and fires to douse." Shelby eyes the white board then heads to the door, shakes her head, "I'll have you added to my calendar for weekly meetings. You will receive an email, shortly." And with that, the director leaves.

John Maxwell does not need to read the note Webber palmed him to know that Stacy Remington's office, his office, is under surveillance. Not only does he not add another thing to the white board, but he also doesn't use his office phone, or send an email. He spends the rest of the day reviewing files and taking copious notes. He is just wrapping up when he receives a cell call from Fred Serpico—he lets it go to voicemail. After another twelve-hour day, John leaves the Federal building with his overstuffed briefcase, and heads to his hotel room. Along the way, he pulls a single-use cell from his pocket and returns Fred's call.

"I saw you called my cell. Did you leave a message?"

"No."

"Good, don't."

"You're being surveilled?"

"Stacy Remington was, so by extension I am. Why did you call?"

"Mason Trellis, assistant chief of Investigative Services for the DC Metropolitan Police Department was killed last night by the Philly PD detective I'm working with. It looks as though Trellis came to finish the assassination of Penny Meehan and got fucked for his troubles. We're running him through RFI, but he's from your neck of the woods, so if you hear anything that might indicate who his friends are, we'd appreciate the assist."

"Done," he disconnects.

Mr. and Mrs. Naught-Naught-Zero.

Randy and Peyton are met at the airport by Rocco and Joy Fiancetti. They jog from the jet that's taxied to a back section of the tarmac and exit through a gated fence. Randy opens a door for Peyton, "Get in, Babe," then sets about brushing snow from the covered vehicle. He shakes the wintry fluff from himself and joins the others, "How long have you been waiting?"

"Twenty minutes or so," Joy smiles, "the snow is coming down at a rapid clip of a couple of inches an hour, there was at least a half-foot when we arrived. We're in for a long ride, so get comfortable."

The trip is slow, slippery, and silent. The farther away from the airport they get, the deeper the snow, and the less treated the roads. Peyton closes her eyes and grabs onto Randy's thigh when a logging truck passes by with barely an inch to spare.

Joy notices the pained expression on Peyton's face, thinks about letting the moment pass, thinks again. "I can see you're experiencing some anxiety, Peyton. We're still a bit away from our destination, perhaps it will help if we talk. You must be curious about all of this, so ask me anything," Joy smiles wide.

"Anything?"

"Anything."

"Did you ever consider building your secret Compound in the Caribbean, or Hawaii, maybe?"

Rocco and Joy are still laughing when they arrive safely at the forested fortress far, far from the Caribbean and Hawaii.

The Kid and The Justice are put up in a cottage very near to Mike's and Annie's. Within the hour, Mike arrives to take Randy to the Computer Center, and Annie comes to introduce herself to Peyton. "Randy will be gone for hours," Annie begins, "do you want some alone time, or would you like some company?"

"Company. If you leave, I'll be forced to crack my law books," The Justice smiles.

"Right. You're at Penn Law. I was at Suffolk before The Realm tried to get me as their cyber slave."

"Do you miss law school?"

"Nope."

"Because you work in the Computer Center." Peyton suggests.

"Nope. I don diving gear when they need me, but I found something I really enjoy, so Rocco and Joy encouraged me to do what I want while I'm here."

"Are you allowed to tell me what you do? Or are you an agent with deadly skills or something?"

Annie laughs big. Her long honey-blonde hair falls forward over her shoulders. She tosses it back and pulls it into a ponytail that she twists, then lets fall away.

"I'm The Compound chef, and so far as I know, I haven't killed anyone with my culinary skills." Annie smiles and continues. "Cooking was a hobby when I first arrived, so I dabbled a bit in the gourmet kitchen at the Main Cottage. Anyway, the hobby became a fascination, which became a passion, which became my job. Of course, I'm also trained in hand to hand combat and can shoot the shit out of any weapon we have, but I'd rather soufflé if you know what I mean. Are you interested in cooking?"

Peyton smiles awkwardly, "No, but the hand to hand combat and shooting the shit out of things just made my panties wet," she admits on a wide smile.

Annie laughs and does the whole hair flipping and ponytail twisting thing again, "I know, right? Come on, I'll take you to the indoor range. It's after hours, so we should have the place to ourselves. I'll tell Mike to meet us there when he's done with Randy."

Computer Center

Mike delivers the new RFI recruit to the Center then cracks up when Randy address Rocco and Joy Fiancetti as, Mr. and Mrs. Naught-Naught-

Zero, then damned near dies of laughter at the next conversation.

"I know I'm in the middle of Forestville and all, but I could be at NASA, what with all this purring hardware. Last time I was this excited I was meeting Malcolm Price."

"Ah, the Dribbling One," Rocco smiles.

Randy spins on his heels, "Tell me you call him that to his face, and I'll cyber slave for you."

Joy fields this one with a hearty laugh, "Rocco does call him that to his face, but be forewarned, 77 has threatened bodily harm to the rest of us if we indulge in that folly."

Randy slices his arm through the air, "Pish, I'm not afraid of Gretchen's husband."

"Ah, the Bleaching One," Rocco smiles.

Randy slaps his hand on his thigh, "Mr. Bond, you just made my day. Now, Mrs. Bond, how about we go for a dive?"

Athletic Center

Mike meets up with Annie and Peyton at the indoor firing range, as was requested.

"Peyton wants to learn," Annie says with a nudge, "She's a fan of Charlie's Angels, so she's gonna be a natural."

Mike groans and begins his spiel, "There are four cardinal safety rules," .... several minutes later, "Okay, ready for a try, Peyton?"

She nods, runs Mike's instructions through her head, and executes them perfectly. She steps away from Mike, turns her body toward the target with her gun hand pointed to the ground, and when she is facing the target, she assumes the perfect extended shooting position, And. Does. Her. Thing.

“Oh, God. You’re channeling an Angel,” Mike groans.

“Of course,” Peyton shrugs.

Annie squeals, “Which Angel are you?”

“Sabrina, of course,” Peyton laughs, “and you’re Kelly, right?”

“Of course,” Annie confirms.

“Of course,” Mike mocks.

Lewisburg

Malcolm checks caller ID before answering, “Hello, Rocco.”

“Mr. Mayor, The Kid’s cyber skills are stellar. Please consider him poached.”

Malcolm warns, “The Kid is a handful.”

“I am hoping as such,” Rocco replies.

Gretchen, who is sitting at the other end of the leather couch feigns a smile when he disconnects, “Randy is one of them now?”

Malcolm runs his hand along her legs, “Partly. Randy will boost his cyber skills and become weapons trained at The Compound, but he will spend most of his time at the satellite RFI location.”

“They have a secondary facility?”

"We have a secondary facility," he smiles w.i.d.e. "When Rocco first mentioned Randy for an RFI position, I asked him about a satellite location at 275. He was completely onboard, so I asked the tenants on the seventh floor to relocate to other living spaces—they are getting a few upgrades for their inconvenience."

Gretchen laughs, "Renovations? At 275? How unusual."

He laughs, "RFI is leaving half of the seventh floor as apartment space. The other half will be converted into a diving center and office space. If that is something you'd approve, Mrs. Mayor."

"Whatever it takes to keep The Kid around."

He nods. He smiles.

DC

Fred is back at Stacy's, and he and Manuel are behind closed doors banging the LNG angle.

"My gut always said the facility in Everett, Massachusetts was central to Leavy's kidnapping. Now, I'm convinced that if we run everything we know all the way through, we will understand what that entry in Granger Mitchell's notes means—the one where Dominque said the kidnapping of FICA Agent Hannah Leavy was 'significant beyond the kidnapping itself.'"

"Do we have enough to run?"

Fred shrugs. "We know that The Realm wanted a cyber huntress. Roland Gaffney tried to get Joy Fiancetti. Dan Shea tried to get Annie Mahoney-Maxwell, and then managed to snatch Hannah Leavy instead. If she hadn't been rescued, she would have been put on an LNG tanker headed to Peru. The mode of transportation and the tanker's destination **are not coincidental**. Leavy was headed to the home country of Antonio Alvarez, a proven associate of The Realm. When RFI was tightening the screws on Dominique, and we told her that we'd protect her baby and keep her in solitary confinement if she gave us names—she gave us names, but..."

Fred moves to the newly replaced window in Stacy's home office for a good long stare. After several minutes of processing he begins, "…Dominique gave us names, but recent events prove that The Realm is still operational. Dominique either gave up **players** and not **leaders**, or we arrested the original leaders, and they have since been replaced. Either way, we need to figure out why Dominique gave us those particular names. Did she want to keep us away from the upper echelon so the organization could stay operational? Or is there some reason she wanted us investigating **those** particular associates? We need to dive deep on those players and their countries of origin. I want to put

Peyton on the LNG angle. No one is better at research, so let's have her research."

Manuel nods, "Peyton Wells is at The Compound with Researcher Randy—who, by the way, Rocco hired to replace John. I'll give Joy a call."

"Yeah. And give her a warning about The Kid."

"Nope. It'll be more fun if Mr. and Mrs. Fiancetti find out about him on their own."

G, C, P, B, C, A, A.

Peyton spends the morning at the firing range and at the hand to hand combat training gym. She hits the showers, grabs some lunch with Annie, then hightails it to the Computer Center to begin her research. Shortly before midnight, Joy joins her, “Are you ready?” The young researcher gives a nod and a Betty Boop smile. Joy gets her onto a secure video conference with Fred and Manuel, listens in, and records their call.

“Okay,” Peyton begins, “I have three areas of note on this subject. I’ll do an information dump before I open it up for questions. First area of note is a little background: LNG is a natural gas extracted from underground rock formations and cooled down to a liquid form. It is more economical than black energy sources like fuel, oil, and diesel. The LNG industry is currently in a boon cycle. Expectations are that liquified natural gas will account for ten percent of global crude production by 2020.

“There is **huge** money in LNG, but the financial gain has been limited to IOCs—International oil companies like Exxon Mobil, Shell, BP, and Chevron. These companies cornered the market very early on by locking 40 countries into importing contracts and 19 countries into exporting contracts. Those arrangements disproportionately benefit the IOCs because the conglomerates set the rate for exporters and the costs for importers. Prior to the freaking fracking explosion in the United States, we were an importing country. When the sea-to-shining-sea-shale-revolution hit America, we no longer needed gas imports. In fact, our abundant gas reserves allowed us to get into the export game in 2016 in a very big way. In a single year, the U.S. became the leading natural gas producer in the world.

"Second area of note is a little review: I want to go back to the roots of the Tango dance. I'm going to explain my thoughts by using three equations that will include my assumptions." Peyton hears a growl from her audience, "They are easy equations, Manuel. And we should discuss why you studied economics if you aren't into equations," she laughs.

"Can do them. Don't like them."

"I'll keep it brief, then. **Number 1**: G, C, P, B, C, A, A = Germany, Czechoslovakia, Poland, Bohemia, Cuba, Africa, and Argentina = the countries of origin of the dance known as Tango. **Number 2**: G, C, P, B, C, A, A = Guatemala, Columbia, Peru, Brazil, Chile, Africa, and Argentina = the countries of origin for the operation known as Tango. **Number 3**: G, C, P, B, C, A, A = Stiles Sigüenza of Guatemala, Miguel Sosa of Columbia, Antonio Alvarez of

Peru, Raphael Ruiz of Brazil, Julio Romero of Chile, Binto Dube of Africa, and Castro López of Argentina = the leaders of Tango, **not** the leaders of The Realm."

Peyton lets that balloon float and burst before continuing. "My research shows the G, C, P, B, C, A, A countries are all major players in LNG imports or exports. Moreover, they are countries that are controlled by IOCs. The countries on the export end see their profits being gobbled up by the fat cats. The countries on the import end see exorbitant levies being imposed by the fat cats. If the Tango program is about LNG, I think it's about getting the G, C, P, B, C, A, A, countries out from under the control of IOCs."

Peyton pauses when she hears a soft guttural growl. "Fred?"

"Yes, Peyton."

"Do you have something to say?"

"I have something to ask."

"Go for it."

"Is the third area of note a way for Tango countries to get out from under the IOCs control?"

"Why, yes it is. Would you like to hear about it, Fred?"

"Yes, Peyton."

"This area of note relates to the arrests of the supposed Realm leaders. There is a before arrest focus and an after arrest focus. I'm going to focus on the after part—it will bring into focus and help explain the before part..."

"Are there equations involved?" Manuel quips.

"No equations."

"Then, you may continue," he laughs.

"Shortly after the supposed Realm leaders were arrested, the US Treasury and Energy departments signed an agreement that allowed private investors to get into the LNG game in South America. There are **huge** LNG opportunities throughout the continent; primarily in countries that aren't under the IOC's contractual thumb, or in those nearing the end of protracted and restrictive contracts with the IOCs. **If** The Realm knew the U.S. was going to allow private investors into a cash cow enterprise, then Tango makes perfect sense. The nefarious organization could put together a subgroup of individuals who have experience in LNG to oversee a financially lucrative program; maybe even name that program Tango.

"Okay, now for the before part of this area of note. Since G, C, P, B, C, A, A are foreign countries, the leaders would have needed someone inside the U.S. government—someone who would know that the U.S. Treasury and Energy departments were getting ready to sign an agreement allowing private investors into the LNG game in South America. A lobbyist would definitely be in the know on something like this. Certainly, the CEO of a gold-standard lobbying firm would know something like this. I'm sure you're all thinking Benton Brettenvue—and you should be. His lobbying chops and his decade long association with Antonio Alvarez places him at the apex of Tango. As a tagalong to Benton is the Pennsylvania Queen of Fracking, Abigail Forrester, who coincidentally, has a long-standing relationship with the 2020 Republican presidential candidate, Turner Rodgers. You put all of these people in the same room and you get a lot of suspicious elbow rubbing. That's all I have at this point, so feel free to have at it."

Rocco Fiancetti speaks for his team, "The detectives and specialists will use the abundance of information you have provided them, Ms. Wells. While they are doing so, you should get some sleep, and then you and I should speak about your future, si?"

"Si, Mr. Bond," Peyton smiles her adorable, bowed lips.

Don't. Fuck. It. Up.

Felicity Ferraro, aka Mrs. Paul Ferraro, aka Irish, is behind closed office doors at the law offices of Preston and Porter. The attorney is not currently toiling for the firm—she gave up that pretense hours ago—she is waiting impatiently for a phone call from Turner Rodgers. Upon her arrival that day, she told her paralegal she did not want to be disturbed, so when a knock comes on her door, she ignores it. When she hears a voice from the other side announce, "Secret Service, ma'am," she stands from her seat.

Presidential candidate Turner Rodgers enters the office and closes the door behind him. "Moments ago, I removed my business from Preston and Porter. I told your senior partners I can no longer be associated with the wife of Paul Ferraro given he is currently behind bars for his involvement in the Stacy Remington assassination. The senior partners of this firm decided they would rather I stay with the firm. Your employment will be terminated as soon as you and I conclude this meeting."

Irish anger is quick to find Felicity. The look on Turner Rodgers' face causes her to quickly tamp it down.

"Your unemployment is a fortuitous circumstance for The Realm. I need to scale back my day to day involvement and focus my efforts on getting elected. You will assume the role of conduit. You will deliver directives to the Gang of Eight and report back to me. As of today, you are The Face of The Realm."

The newly promoted operative does not throw a blush, bat an eye, crack a smile, or furrow a brow. Turner Rodgers' words elicit no outwardly reaction. That's because Felicity Ferraro is a brilliant and ruthless woman who is perfectly capable of being second in line to The Body. Still, she knows the appointment is going to be problematic," The Gang of Eight will go ballistic."

He nods. "The Gang will not take kindly to your promotion given that they want you gone from the organization. The only reason they haven't made a move against you is because you have the goods on them. I warned them that the 'fixer' always has the goods—always marks a trail—always sets a trap. Individually, you own each of their asses, but make no mistake, Felicity, if they band together, they will break you—then they will kill you."

Felicity stiffens her back and smiles w.i.d.e. "Please tell The Gang I am an O'Brennan. If they are unfamiliar with that reference tell them to research the Irish insurrection known as Easter Rising. Then tell them they may very well kill me, but they will **never** break me. You might also want to remind them I have the goods on more than the Gang of Eight," she pauses, "and if need be, I will destroy the whole of DC—whether I be dead or alive."

Turner Rodgers takes the prick of that slung arrow, "Is that a threat?"

"Of course not."

He begins putting her into her place, "Some will question your promotion given your recent fuckups."

She strolls her office, comes to a stop at the bank of windows that overlook DC, "Those were Paul's fuckups."

"Not much separation between you two, Felicity. I'd say it's no more than a dick's worth. You need to listen very carefully to the rest of what I have to say." He joins her at the window and blocks her movements. "This is where The Realm currently stands. There is major fallout from the assassination of Stacy Remington. John Maxwell has taken over FICA. His being in the director's seat is worse than when Remington was there. Shit does not get past John Maxwell. He is a problem that needs taking care of at a time when we are down two contract killers. We've got one killer sitting his ass in jail, and the other with his ass in a morgue. I don't give a fuck about either of them. This is what I give a fuck about, the Dominique and Celia

Brettenvue files are not in our possession, and the investigative reporter who's been nosing into my life is not in a fucking grave."

He steps closer. She stands her ground. He leans in. "Your promotion has three immediate consequences. The first is that you are no longer involved in arranging or overseeing contract hits. The second and third are a combo gift to you; someone else is handling assassinations now, the new guy, or gal, might take out your husband—or you. That would result in four little Ferraro orphans."

Felicity tries to move past Turner.

"Stay where you are."

She stays where she is.

"My eyes and ears inside the walls say that your husband is threatening to talk if you don't get your ass to the jail to see him. Paul has become a liability—you know what happens to liabilities. I haven't deemed Paul useless and expendable, yet. So, it's time for you to get your ass to the jail, find out what Paul plans to do, then do **whatever** you have to do to calm him down. Have I made myself clear?"

She nods.

The presidential candidate steps away, "Sit, Felicity, there's business to attend. I called a meeting with the Gang of Eight for tomorrow night. It will be the first meeting that you will conduct. The Gang will want explanations and reassurances. You're only going to get one chance to assuage them and exert power over them, so Don't. Fuck. It. Up."

"I have an organizational question."

"What is it?"

"Now that Tango is behind us, is the main objective of The Realm the same as it's always been? Are we going after Joy Fiancetti, Annie Mahoney-Maxwell and Hannah Leavy?"

"Yes." Turner walks to the door and stops. "Convince your husband to shut the fuck up."

Felicity stays standing until Turner Rodgers leaves her office. As soon as he is through the door, she drops her ass back onto her chair.

That's the link.

Fred Serpico got up on the wrong side of the bed. By the time the sun joined him, he'd already spent hours standing at an ink-black window processing the shit out of something. He is now rummaging through an overstuffed carrying bag, for the third time. He growls in frustration when he finally grabs hold of a stack of papers that had escaped earlier discovery. He slaps them onto Stacy's desk.

"It's always in the last place you look," he grouses.

"What's always in the last place you look?" Manuel asks from the doorway.

"Whatever it is you're looking for—you always find it in the last place you look."

"Well, yeah. Why would you keep looking for something after you found it?"

"What are you looking for?" Leavy asks.

"The point of this fucking conversation," Fred grouses.

Leavy turns to leave, "What the hell crawled up his butt?"

Fred calls out after her, "Sorry about that. How are you feeling?"

"Antsy. I need something to do."

"Good. Can you look through the research you did on military personnel? I want to see if there's a connection between Paul Ferraro and Mason Trellis that precedes their association with The Realm."

"Go put on some coffee, Fred. And Manuel, give me Stacy's computer codes," she says as she takes a seat at the desk. The cyber huntress has made some headway by the time the men return. "Mason Trellis was a former Army Ranger who trained Paul Ferraro before retiring from the military. Not sure if they kept in contact throughout all of the years, but Trellis was an original financial backer of and instructor at Ferraro's survivalist training schools."

Fred claps his hands, "That's the link. Thanks, Leavy."

Washington

Felicity Ferraro is in a meeting room at the DC Correctional Treatment Facility awaiting the arrival of her client, who is also her husband. While she waits, she paces—while she paces, she counsels herself, "The stakes are high. You need to convince him that you stayed away because you've been working on his defense." She is interrupted by a knock on the door and the entrance of a correctional officer, "Please take a seat, Attorney Ferraro, and remain seated. Do not touch the prisoner in any way during your meeting."

She takes her seat.

He takes her breath away.

The man who enters the room is physically maimed and emotionally strained. The arm that received the shoulder wound is folded into a sling and the hand that took a bullet does not resemble a hand anymore. Though still heavily bandaged, Felicity can see that it is missing two fingers and hangs freely, as though it is no longer attached to his wrist. No words are exchanged while the prisoner is unchained, seated, and rechained.

"Where the hell have you been, Felicity?"

"Well, Paul, I've been mothering our children, and dealing with the fallout of them finding out about you. Oh, and I've been fighting for my job, so I can defend you in court." By the time she finishes her outburst, she is glaring at him.

"Seems I got your Irish up, wifey."

She ignores him, reaches into her briefcase and pulls a legal pad and pen. "We should get to your case, Paul."

"What, no questions about how I'm doing?"

Felicity refolds her arms across her chest and leans back against her seat, "I have eyes, Paul, I can see how you are doing. Now, if you expect me to mount a proper defense for you, you'd better stop wasting the time we have."

"The only thing you'll be mounting, Felicity, is my dick."

She pulls a deep breath, "Are you finished?"

"For now. I hope you figured out that the case against me will never see the inside of a courtroom. There will be no defense—because there will be no prosecution."

"And why is that?"

"A prosecution case depends on witness testimony. Dead witnesses can't testify."

Attorney Ferraro leans forward, "Killing witnesses and informants hasn't been your strong-suit lately. I hope you have a backup plan."

He smiles his Bradley Cooper smile, "How's a presidential pardon for a backup plan?"

She wants to say it's unlikely he'll get one, but she simply smiles and changes the subject. "Mason Trellis is dead."

"He's better off in a morgue than in here. What happened?"

"He was in Philly trying to finish your fuckup on Penny Meehan."

"It wasn't a fuckup—she was shot—she just didn't die."

"As I was saying, he was cut down at the hands of Meehan's boyfriend, Detective Brothers."

Paul laughs, "Are you sure that's how it went down, Felicity?"

"What's that supposed to mean?"

"If The Realm wanted Trellis dead, that's the story they'd be telling—**after** they put a bullet through his head. I'm sure they'll have quite the story when they kill me—and you."

"You're paranoid, Paul."

"You'd better be, Felicity."

Somewhere in DC

The Gang of Eight have been waiting nearly an hour for Felicity Ferraro. Their outward hostility hits her full when she walks into the room. She ignores it.

"Turner will not be joining us this evening, or for the foreseeable future. He is stepping back his involvement and focusing his efforts on his campaign which as we all know is vital to the success of The Realm. That decision has resulted in an organizational change. Turner has appointed me as his conduit."

FBI Deputy Director Jack Johnson is the first to challenge her, "Why you?"

"Our boss has his reasons."

Jack angers instantly. "This is no time for Turner to be taking a back seat. There are two high-profile investigations underway, thanks to the fuckup assassins **you** managed, Mrs. Ferraro. Let's recap, shall we? Mason Trellis was killed at the home of Philly Detective Ted Brothers. There are a lot of people who want to know why a DC gold-badge cop was in Drexel Hill, Pennsylvania, and whether his middle-of-the-night visit had anything to do with the woman reporter who survived an assassination attempt by your fuckup husband. The person who **really** wants to know about that is RFI super-sleuth Fred Serpico. Given that he's living inside Stacy Remington's goddamn house, there's a good chance he's gonna find the answers to that question, and a whole lot more. I've put him under surveillance, but Serpico is with RFI. He didn't get there without knowing how to slip and slide through and around a few sets of eyes. Now, let's discuss the Paul Ferraro legendary fuckup. Who on God's green earth could shoot a short, black woman instead of a tall, white man? I don't care what her movements were, and what the circumstances in the tree line were, that assassination was a major fuckup. I'm inside the Bureau, and the whole fucking place is in an uproar over this. Every goddamn one of the Gang of Eight might feel a cold breeze from Paul's fuckup, but the fiercest winds are hitting closest to me. Now that Stacy's dead, I've got John Maxwell sitting in the office next to mine. For Christ's sake, Mrs. Ferraro, what makes Turner think this is the time to step back, or that any one of us will support **you** as his conduit?"

"I do not favor your support, Jack, but I do demand your fealty. When I leave here tonight and the lot of you start entertaining ways to get rid of me, keep this in mind. I do not dither in threats, I take action, and my actions will destroy every last one of you." The Face turns and walks out the door.

Turner Rodgers is on the phone with Felicity before she makes it to her car, "You've bought yourself some time. Use it wisely." He disconnects and is back on the phone a minute later, "Now what?" he asks The Body.

There is a lengthy pause before The Body speaks. "Tell your new conduit to ride Jack Johnson. He needs to up the surveillance on the RFI members. We need to know where they are every second of every day. We will neutralize Maxwell, Serpico, and Xavier when we make a move on cyber huntress Leavy."

Coed showers and root cellars.

Joy Fiancetti was in and out of the FBI systems in record time. She was defended masterfully by Randy. "You remind me of a young John Maxwell," Joy says to the beaming Kid.

"Mrs. Bond, I gladly accept that compliment."

Joy places a call to Fred, "I'm sending the information you requested. Safeguard it."

"With my life," he assures her.

Fred passes by the Reynolds brothers on his way out of Stacy Remington's place. Eli eyes Fred's gear, "Looks like he's leaving, brother. Do you think we should check his bags, make sure he's not lifting some of Stacy's things?"

Fred smacks Eli on the shoulder, "I'll be back to pilfer at a later date. Although, technically, I am stealing Stacy's wheels."

"Those aren't Stacy's wheels, Fred. Technically, you're stealing a Federal vehicle. Not to worry, though, I am a skilled attorney, if you find you need one," Mathis banters.

Fred smiles and calls over his shoulder. "Good to know."

Fred calls Ted Brothers from the road, "Hey, Theodore. I need a place to crash and work for a few days. I've got some files that no one can know about."

"What's your ETA, Fred?"

"Dinnertime."

"Don't come by way of the breezeway," Ted laughs big.

DC

FICA Director John Maxwell ignores the call that is patched through to him. When there is a knock on the door, he ignores that, too. When his assistant, Agent Amanda Rhys, pokes her head into the office, John barely raises his head from the files he's reading.

"Excuse my interruption, but there is an urgent matter, Director Maxwell," Agent Rhys walks a note to her boss. He reads it. **Philadelphia field office on line 4: Director Remington's vehicle pulled over outside city limits by Philly PD. Fred Serpico is resisting arrest. He is in handcuffs and is threatening legal action if the vehicle is searched.**

John answers the flashing line on his phone, "This is FICA Director Maxwell, with whom am I speaking?"

"Agent Terrence Gordon, sir."

"Agent Gordon, there is a problem, and you are going to fix it. The operator of that vehicle is on a case contracted out of this office.

He has been loaned the Federal vehicle that I understand is currently sitting on the side of the road. This circumstance is preventing him from doing his job. Care to explain?"

"A Philly highway patrol officer pulled the vehicle over because it was called in as a stolen vehicle and because the driver was speeding, sir."

"The vehicle is not stolen; it is on loan. If the Philly PD wants to issue a speeding citation, let the officer do so, but the driver should be sent on his way. Agent Gordon, the vehicle should not be searched, and I expect the operator of the vehicle to be on his way in three minutes. Am I clear?"

"Yes, sir."

"Very good. Tell the patrol officer I expect a call from the operator in four minutes. Am I clear?"

"Yes, sir."

Fred calls John's cell phone in two minutes.

John lets it go to voicemail.

Drexel Hill

Fred arrives at Ted's long after dinner. He is pissed, he is hungry, and he is determined to find out who the fuck tracked him and tried to fuck him.

"Ted, if that vehicle had been searched, I'd be spending the rest of my days at Leavenworth.

Someone has me in their sights. I shouldn't stay here. If this place gets raided, we'll all end up in Federal prison."

"As long as Ted and I are cellmates, I'm good, Fred."

"No co-ed showers inside a penitentiary, Lucky," Ted teases.

"In that case, we'd better hide the files, Fred."

"Follow me. Both of you." Ted leads them to the area just inside the front door. To one side is the den—to the other is his office addition—between the two is a small wall section covered by paneling. He reaches to the top and flips a hidden lever. The section clicks open, "Root cellar," he smiles, "go on down, Fred. I'll stay here with Penny."

Fred returns with a wide smile, "That's quite the setup. I get the office space, but the workspace, what's that used for?"

"Janelle used to make jewelry. That was her space. It should suit you well enough. It might get a little cold, but no one will know you or your files are there once the door is closed behind you."

"I saw a space heater," Fred says.

"Right. I forgot about that. Then you're all set. Why don't you grab your work gear and put it downstairs, just in case we have unexpected visitors. Then head up and put your other gear in the guest bedroom. I'll set you a plate of food."

Penny touches Ted's cheek, "I'm gonna get back to reviewing the files Fred brought on Celia and Dominique."

Ted runs his hand down her arm and gently squeezes her hand, "I'll be in to help as soon as the beast is fed."

Fred notices the change in his friends' touches.

May I speak freely, ma'am?

Agent Amanda Rhys knocks on John Maxwell's door for the second time that day. She enters at his request, walks to his desk, and hands him an envelope.

"Thank you, Agent." John waits for his assistant to leave, she stays put, "Is there something else, Agent?"

"Yes, sir. Please read the correspondence and accept or decline. I will deliver your message, sir."

John reads the correspondence, "I accept."

"Very good, sir," Agent Rhys says, then leaves.

Virginia
FBI Director Shelby Webber lives south of DC on the Potomac River. To be precise Shelby Webber lives in the historic center of Alexandria known as Old Town.

John pulls up to a nineteenth century, three-story, brick home with oversized, multi-paned, black shuttered windows and an arched front doorway. Twin chimneys reach beyond the roof, trimmed with exquisite Dentil crown molding. On the left side of the main structure is a two-story slope-roofed structure. The stately home is surrounded by wrought iron fencing, a section of which swings inward after he announces his arrival.

He parks his government issued vehicle and walks toward the waterfront, pauses for a view of the river, then turns toward the house. He sees Director Webber watching him from a corner to corner bank of windows overlooking the Potomac. She points to an entrance beneath the windows. He enters and follows a set of stairs upward to find his boss standing at the top wearing a UConn long-sleeve T-shirt, a pair of jeans, and so far as he can tell, little else.

"Come on in. Have you had dinner Director Maxwell?"

"No, ma'am."

"Good, I'm serving lasagna. I worked from home today and whenever I work from home, I cook. You're in for a treat—my lasagna is the best, or so I've been told. My sister says that people who find me objectionable invite me to their dinner parties if I'll agree to bring my lasagna. I choose to take that as a compliment." The director heads to the gourmet kitchen that is a huge swath of the open floor space. "Have a look around, the views are wonderful, even in late November."

John walks the artfully arranged space that boasts overstuffed leather couches and mission-style recliners arranged conversational-style facing a mahogany mantled brick fireplace.

Simple, but sturdy end tables, a coffee table, and sideboard, all trimmed in hammered wrought iron finish the seating area. The power of the room is cut by cream colored leather upholstery, rugs, and throw pillows. Off to the side, nestled into a corner facing the Potomac, sits a kitschy arrangement of Adirondack lounge chairs and rockers that have been moved indoors for the winter. He is headed that way when his boss enters the area holding two glasses of red wine.

"There are two constants in my life, Director Maxwell. The first is peering out these windows whenever time permits. The second is an annual trip to Tuscany—or more precisely a trip to the Tenuta Il Poggione vineyard. Tonight, I'm serving the vineyard's Brunello di Montalcino 2014." The director points to the Adirondacks, "Sit, please."

John waits until she is seated in a rocker, then stretches out on a lounge chair. He takes a sip of the wine she handed off. He nods his head, "Very nice."

"I agree. It is very nice. Tell me why you think so."

He clears his throat.

She offers a bit of clarity, "When I retire, I plan on buying into this vineyard. I think its good practice to find out what people think about the wine they are drinking. Indulge me."

"The color is beautiful, and it smells fruity and floral. It has a warmth that is very subtle. And I want to follow the first sip with another."

"Very nicely done. I'd ask for more description, but I think that may be what my friends and family find objectionable about me." She rocks forward and gets up from her seat, "While I finish dinner prep, please enjoy the wine and the views."

The director heads to the kitchen.

John enjoys a sip of the Brunello di Montalcino and the view of her ass as she walks away. He lets memories of their first encounter drift in…

He bumped into her—literally bumped into her—as he was taking the stairs at J. Edgar. He stopped to help her gather her belongings, had his hand swatted away for his troubles, "Confidential material. Leave them where they are and proceed. Perhaps you could pay attention when you corner."

"Yes, ma'am," he laughed on his way past. "She's a doppelganger of Meryl Streep, the bitchy one in something with Prada," he smirked.

John's thoughts pull him dangerously close to the hair washing scene between Meryl Streep's character, Karen Blixen, and Robert Redford's character, Denys Finch Hatton in the movie *Out of Africa*, a scene John considers the height of sensuality.

"Director Maxwell. Director Maxwell!"

John turns toward the voice.

"I see you've become captivated by the views of the Potomac, but dinner is ready."

John cautions himself as he moves toward the kitchen, "Keep your head in the game, and you penis in your pants."

As dinner nears its end, the director does the whole *The Devil Wears Prada* thing on John.

"I heard about Fred Serpico's detainment along the side of a Philadelphia highway."

John raises a brow.

"Agent Rhys works for you Maxwell, but she reports to me."

"Yes, ma'am."

"Serpico was unyielding about having his vehicle searched."

"Yes, ma'am."

"Do you know why that is?"

"I believe so, ma'am."

"Director Maxwell, you are a former member of RFI, but you play on my team now."

"Yes, ma'am."

"Let me try my question, again. Do you know why Fred Serpico was unyielding about having his vehicle searched?"

"Yes, ma'am."

She waits for more. She gets nothing for her trouble. "It appears you are straddling the line of loyalty, Director."

He remains quiet.

She does not.

"Are you aware that I removed your predecessor, Stacy Remington, from all cases related to The Realm?"

"Yes, ma'am."

"Stacy continued her work on the side."

"Yes, ma'am."

"Director Maxwell. I believe she lost her life because of that work." Shelby Webber stares at John knowing damned well he's piecing a few things together.

He gets up and moves about—until he gets the totality of IT. "Ma'am, are you suggesting Granger Mitchell was not the intended target that night and Stacy Remington was?"

Shelby Webber drills a staring hole at the questioner. John holds her stare. After a minute she addresses her subordinate, "Director Maxwell, I am going to ask three questions. I already know the answers to each of them. I suggest you answer truthfully."

"Yes, ma'am."

"One: When Joy Fiancetti hacked into the FBI systems last evening, did she do a deep dive on Turner Rodgers? Two: Does Fred Serpico have that information? Three: Is that the reason for his adamant refusal for a search of his vehicle?"

"Yes, ma'am, to all three questions, ma'am."

"Did you participate in the dive?"

"No, ma'am."

Shelby Webber stares intently at John Maxwell before continuing. "You are aware the office you occupy is still under surveillance."

"Yes, ma'am."

"After today's events with Fred Serpico, it appears that Stacy's government issued vehicle is GPS trapped."

"Yes, ma'am."

"Thoughts, Director Maxwell?"

"Yes, ma'am. May I speak freely?"

Webber nods.

"I'll circle back to the bombshell you just dropped, but first—when you fired RFI and bumped the Celia Brettenvue and Abigail Forrester cases down to the Philly PD, the general assumption at RFI was that you wanted Director Remington off the cases because you were working against the Bureau and protecting The Realm."

The FBI Director folds her arms across her chest, and her foot takes to stomping air—John considers pulling back. "Continue," she directs.

"If that general assumption is incorrect ..."

The Director shifts in her seat, "Maxwell, you are getting very close to seeing me pissed off."

"Yes, ma'am. Let me rephrase that. Since that general assumption **is** incorrect, and you removed Stacy Remington to shield her, then you must believe there is a mole in your ranks and the mole is high enough to surveil the FICA Director, and is connected enough to cause her jeopardy."

Shelby Webber nods.

"Are you willing to name names, Director Webber?"

"Deputy Director Jack Johnson," she answers immediately.

John and Shelby sit with that information for a few minutes.

"May I speak, Director Webber."

She nods.

"Ma'am, if Jack Johnson was surveilling Remington at the office, and there is a GPS trap on her car, then he must have put eyes and ears in Stacy's home office. That's most likely where she did her work once you sidelined her."

The Director shakes her head, "Stacy was vigilant in keeping ahead of surveillance. I'm quite sure she swept her home several times each day, however..."

John interrupts his boss. "The RFI team has been working out of Stacy's house for days. Their work is being compromised."

"I suggest you call Fred Serpico, Director Maxwell. He's at Ted Brothers' place in Drexel."

Watch Leavy!

Jack Johnson pulls his vehicle into the heavy tree line a quarter-mile from Director Webber's house. He trains his binoculars on the wall of windows that overlook the Potomac. "Nice setting. Particularly advantageous that your place sits on a little inlet. Gives me the perfect view." He hones in on the farmer's table, "Mmm, lasagna. Looks good. Speaking of looking good .... Shelby .... Webber .... you sure do unwind nicely. Damn, you look like a college coed in that sweatshirt and pair of jeans .... and your hair, all soft and sexy. Are you doing Maxwell?" He'd no sooner uttered those words when John Maxwell got up and left the kitchen. "Wait a minute, he didn't just leave the upstairs, he went outside .... to make a call .... he wanted privacy? From his boss?" Jack opened his computer, "Let's see who you're calling .... nothing .... Maxwell's using a burner." The Deputy Director of the FBI shuts his computer, tosses his binoculars on the seat, and leaves.

Drexel Hill
Fred, Ted and Penny are in the kitchen waiting for the second pot of coffee to perk when Fred receives a call from John Maxwell. He begins a

slow roil, then amps up to a seething anger, as he listens and paces the tight space.

“Fuck it all, John. I knew **you** were being surveilled at the Bureau, but Stacy’s dead, there’s no reason to surveil her office ……. fuck it all, John, I’m on it.”

Ted and Penny wait as Fred places a call, “Leavy, talk to me as though I’m Gretchen.”

The sound of Fred’s voice puts Leavy on alert. “Just hanging out. I’m actually grabbing a few minutes alone.”

“Good. Your place is heavily surveilled. Get Manuel outside. Bring your phone and earbuds. I’ll call back in five minutes.”

“That sounds wonderful. Let me talk with Manuel and Fred about it. Okay, say hello to Malcolm, and give 78 a little pat from Auntie Leavy.” She disconnects from the call that Fred has long since ended.

Leavy arrives downstairs with her hat, coat, and mittens on. “Oh, good, you’re still here, Eli. I’m desperate for some fresh air. Is it okay if I go for a little walk?”

Eli bounds to his feet, “Yes, but not alone. I could use some air—I’ll come with,” he says with a wide grin.

Manuel growls, “Back down, doctor.” In seconds Manuel is ready to take his woman for a walk. They open the front door to tiny, dancing snowflakes and greeted by Leavy's happy squeal. "I love snow! Cannot get enough snow!"

Leavy ignores the first vibrating call from Fred. When she and Manuel have turned a corner, she hands Manuel her phone and earbuds. "Put these in. Fred's calling."

He buds up and takes the call. "Fred? What's going on?"

"Stacy's house is heavily surveilled, and her FBI Escalade is GPS trapped. I was stopped heading to Philly, handcuffed for resisting arrest, and the SUV was almost searched. Someone dropped a dime that the Escalade was stolen. If John hadn't gotten me out of the mess, I'd be in Leavenworth as we speak, and I don't think they'd let me take the stuff we have on Rodgers inside."

"Plan?" Manuel asks.

"We use the surveillance to our advantage. You and Leavy go low with your work and your words. Mathis and Eli are around enough you can casually talk about the case with them, to give the eyes and ears something, but keep it to logistics – who will be where when, that sort of thing. We've been talking too much already, but Mathis doesn't seem too surprised at things we say—husbands and wives usually hear things they aren't supposed to. The thing is, the Reynolds brothers might be in a bit of danger if the eyes and ears think they know things, but I've been doing a mental review of what we've said in their company and nothing jumps out as being anything that's not already in the public. The stuff from Peyton on LNG, Mathis and Eli weren't in earshot, but whoever's surveilling us got an ear full. When you get back inside, don't let on about the surveillance, the brothers might tighten up, and inadvertently tip off the snoops."

Manuel jumps in, "Fred, I was thinking — if Tango is what Peyton thinks it is, a financial program — and the real leaders of The Realm aren't behind bars — then the organization's original goals are still in play — that means the cyber huntresses are in danger."

"Fuck, Manuel, we need to lock Leavy down. Get her back to Stacy's. Don't freak the brothers out. Use them as unwitting guards, until I can get Mike down here. Expect him in hours."

"Before you go, Fred. Did John have any ideas about who might be behind the surveilling?"

"Deputy Director of the FBI Jack Johnson for starters. And Manuel, that information was given to John by FBI Director Shelby Webber. I need to call Rocco. Watch Leavy!"

Manuel disconnects from Fred's call, leans back against one of two brick columns that begins the brick walkway leading to Stacy's front door. He wraps his arms around Leavy's waist, gets lost in thought…

"Former Agent Xavier, this is Director Remington."

"Good morning, ma'am. What is the status on your communication, ma'am?"

"Secure line."

"Very well, ma'am … It's my understanding that you've been working from home, Director."

"Yes."

"Surveillance issues at J. Edgar, ma'am?"

"Yes."

"And at your home?"

"I've been scanning daily…"

"Before we proceed further, what is your current communication status?"

"Secure line."

"Yes, ma'am. Maxwell just confirmed that."

Manuel pulls Leavy against him and pecks her cheek and lips. Then he wraps his arms tight, "We are heavily surveilled inside. When we go in, we spend some time with the brothers, then we head to the shower. I'll tell you then what's going on." Manuel ends his talk with a deep, passionate kiss. "Leavy, look at me. I want you to know that I am deeply, passionately in love with you."

Leavy gets it, "The Realm is after me again?" she whispers.

Manuel nods.

Steel drums and panic attacks.

When Leavy returns from her walk, she is invigorated and flushed rosy-pink. Within minutes, she does a fake quick dip into exhaustion. Doctor Eli checks a few things out, then suggests that she call it a night; she and Manuel willingly oblige. By the time they arrive in the master bedroom, he is desperate—to hold her—to be inside her—to keep her safe. He gets the shower all warm and steamy, then goes back to the bedroom to get Leavy. He finds her standing in front of a window, deeply lost in thought…

Leavy was thrown into the back of the kidnapper's vehicle, quickly blindfolded, silenced by tape slapped across her mouth, and bound with tape wrapped around her wrists. There was no conversation between her kidnappers. She used the silence to run the kidnapping scene through her head.

Three cars approached me. Two masked kidnappers got out of their cars and grabbed me. They left their cars at the farmhouse. All three kidnappers are in this car. One is in the back with me.

She concentrated on the length of time she was on the road and calculated that the trip lasted an hour before the vehicle came to a stop.

She didn't resist when she was dragged into a musty building that had a cavernous feel to it. *Sounds take a long time to return.* Her handlers threw her onto some sort of cushion. *A mattress.* Leavy knew the men were standing around her, but no one spoke. Until he arrived.

"FICA Agent Hannah Leavy. It is good to see you again."

Dan Shea. The – penny – dropped. *He's taken me as a replacement for DOA and the Girl Genius, I am The Realm's cyber huntress.*

~

Leavy was down on a mattress inside the cavernous room. She was cold and hungry, and her left side was numb from lying on it for hours. She wasn't afraid of what was happening to her right then. She knew that Shea and his men wouldn't hurt her, or kill her, because they needed her. Leavy was afraid of what would happen to her once she was turned over to The Realm. She knew that she would be forced to go to the dark side and was fully aware of the methods the nefarious ones would use to get her there. A mantra started in the captive woman's head, and whispered from her lips. "Fiat lux, let there be light. Fiat lux, let there be light. Fiat lux, let there be light." UC Berkeley's motto—Leavy's valedictorian speech. That was the tie that would bind her to the goodness of light as she was forced toward the dark side.

~

Four men in an LNG-labeled field truck pulled next to the kidnapper's vehicle. The men got out of the truck, each one carrying a large fully packed duffle bag. The kidnapper lowered the window, inspected the contents of each duffle, and nodded to the leader. The bearded man directed, "Get it." His men returned to the LNG truck, pulled down the tailgate, rolled a steel drum toward them, and when it hit the ground, it did so with a metallic-sounding thud. They rolled it toward the car. The leader tossed the duffle bags onto the back seat of the Subaru, leaned into the car and spoke softly to the woman who was on the floor wedged between the front and back seats. "You are being put into a steel drum and transported to a tanker that will take you out of the country. There is plenty of room for you inside. If you make a sound, I will seal the drum tight until you are on the tanker. Stay quiet, and I will leave the top open. Do you understand what I am telling you?"

Leavy nodded. She pushed back against a lifetime of claustrophobic fear, and didn't resist when she was pulled from the car and lowered into the drum, which was then lifted and put onto the LNG truck. When the kidnapper left the parking lot, the transport truck was moved to the side of an abandoned building. A chain-link fence overgrown with bushes and vines obscured the truck from view. The leader made a call from his cell. "Come," was all he said before getting out of the truck. He surveyed the area around him then lowered the tailgate and jumped onto the flatbed. He lifted off the top of the drum, reached inside, and pulled Leavy up by her bound wrists to a standing position. "You are safe, for now. Follow my directions explicitly. Do you understand, Agent Leavy?"

She nodded.

Agent Manuel Xavier removed Agent Hannah Leavy's blindfold. When her eyes adjusted to the breaking light of day, recognition flooded, "You're FBI," she croaked.

"Yes."

"You're undercover in The Realm?"

"Until this morning, yes. Once they realize I have taken the cyber huntress known as 2.0, they will realize my duplicity. I am a dead man if they catch me. You are a dead woman if they catch you. I suggest we work together to make sure they don't catch us. Come, our ride should be here any minute."

"Leavy." Manuel moves toward her, "Leavy, where are you?"

"Inside a fucking steel drum."

He pulls her to him, "No. You are here with me." He kisses the top of her head as she nestles it onto his chest. They stay locked in an embrace for several minutes before heading to the shower.

Manuel intends to tender his woman—she lets him know she has other plans in mind. She moves her man against the shower wall and dominates him. Her touches are urgent and purposeful. She demands his kisses then trails some down to the length of him. She takes the full of him into her mouth and quickly works him to the edge.

Manuel reaches down and pulls her to her feet, “Leavy, what’s going on?”

“I need .... I need.” Leavy’s desire is tangled with fear and anger. She pushes away from Manuel and walks from the shower. “I need some time alone.” She wraps herself in a bathrobe, heads downstairs, and runs full force into Eli, “Sorry,” she says as she moves past.

Eli grabs her hand before she moves completely out of reach, “Leavy, what’s wrong?”

“Nothing,” she says avoiding his eyes.

“Are you feeling ill? You seem angry. Unless there is a reason for your anger, then it may be a residual from your concussion. I don’t want to pry, but is your level of anger justified?”

“Gee, I don’t know Eli. Are flashbacks of being put into a steel drum with the prospect of being held against my will for the rest of my life justification for the level of anger I’m currently feeling?”

Eli pulls her into an embrace, “I am crossing a line here, Leavy, but you need to be held through this.”

She struggles to get free.

He holds tight.

She struggles herself right into a fit of tears.

He holds tight.

She drops to her knees.

He follows.

She releases a torrent of tears that wash away her fear and anger and leave her spent.

He stands and offers her his hand, "Leavy, I'm sorry you went through all that. You can't hold the residuals of your kidnapping in because they will bring you to your knees again. I'm not telling you things you don't already know."

She nods.

"I suspect you've had this type of episode already, which means you know the triggers. Did something happen to bring you to this place tonight?"

"Nothing specific. I think I was getting unsettled earlier, that's why I wanted to go for a walk. To be honest, Eli, I think this episode hit because I've been cooped up, you know like being in a steel drum."

Leavy and Eli are interrupted by Mathis who enters the kitchen through the pantry wall. "Brother? Leavy? Is all well?"

Leavy sends a thank you look to Eli, walks past Mathis and touches his arm, "It is now, thanks to Eli. If you two will excuse me, I've left my man upstairs in a rather confused state. Good night."

Manuel is standing in front of the window Leavy vacated several moments before. He turns when she enters the room and waits for her approach.

"Manuel, I want you to take me, control me, press me deep. I need to feel what's here, between us. I need to stay out of my head. Please, Manuel."

He stalks toward her, pushes her onto the bed and presses into her. He brings her close, then pulls back. He ignores her pleas for release until he can take it no longer. When every ounce of them is shared, he keeps his full weight on top of her. When her breathing becomes shallow and fitful, and her tears come, he rolls from her.

"Leavy, I was the one who put you in that drum. That fact must be part of your flashbacks. It can't be good for you that we've never addressed my role in your kidnapping. I think you jump past that part of the horror and go to the part where I pulled you to freedom. Leavy, when you start going through your flashbacks, go through the whole event. Accept that it was me, that I participated in what hurts you now, then remember I pulled you from that danger. I will always protect you, Leavy—even if it's with my dying breath. Tell me you know that, please."

"I do know Manuel, but it doesn't bring me comfort."

Bye, bye, Benny.

Layne Osterman of Beaver Falls has spent more than a month hiking the back woods of Pennsylvania and sweating the sheets with Benton Brettenvue, now known as Benny Terrio. They are sharing his no-tell-motel bed when she is woken by a vibrating cell phone. She pulls it from beneath her pillow, checks caller ID, and slides from bed. From behind a closed bathroom door, she whispers, "It's been awhile."

"The organization is restructuring. I'm your boss now. We're down two assassins, so you're being bumped up."

"Yes, sir."

"I need you in Philadelphia to take out two people."

"Yes, sir."

"Get rid of Brettenvue, first. We don't need him. Let me know when you're in Philly. Two days tops, Osterman."

"Yes, sir."

Layne gently opens the bathroom door—Benny is waiting for her on the other side.

"Who were you talking to?" he snarls.

"My Daddy," Layne says as she tries to move past him.

"At three in morning?" he blocks her exit.

"He's stink-ass drunk and going on about all the time I'm taking away from the store. Even drunk, the old coot has a point. I come home after a three-month stay in Alaska and immediately shack up with you. I've barely set foot in the store since the day you came in to buy all your gear. I listened to the old man's rage, then agreed to work for the next few days."

Layne tries to get past Benton, again. He doesn't budge. "I've explained about the call, Benny, now step the fuck back, you're starting to piss me off."

"Good, I like a bitch who fights back."

"Then you're gonna love this." Before his next blink, she knees him in the balls, jumps over him as he drops, pulls his head back by his hair, places one arm around his neck and her dominant hand across his forehead, lifts herself up to get leverage, then twists Benton Brettenvue's head to coincide with her downward trajectory. Layne hears and feels the snap, lets him fall dead away, then checks his jugular. "You should have stepped out of my way, Benny." She hops over his body, pulls a dress on over her head, a pair of boots onto her feet, grabs her things, hangs the *No Maid Service* tag on the outside motel door, grabs the keys to Benny's Camaro, and gets the fuck out of Beaver Falls.

As soon as she is beyond the town limits she calls her Daddy.

"It's 3 AM, Sugar, someone better be dead."

"Someone is. Room 11 at the motel. The body needs to disappear, along with my Tahoe,"

"I'm on it, Sugar. You heading out?"

"Already on the road. I'll be in touch when I can, Daddy. Thanks for the help." Layne disconnects that call and makes another, "Sarge. It's Osterman. I could use some help."

"You found my phone number, Osterman, I'm sure you can find my place."

Drexel Hill

Fred Serpico has been holed up in the root cellar workroom at Ted Brothers' log cabin for hours trying to push through the voluminous file on Turner Rodgers. Now that he's arranged for Mike Monopoli to join Manuel and Leavy at Stacy's townhouse, he can focus on this part of the investigation. When he heads upstairs for lunch, Penny fills him in on the part she's been working on.

"I've read and reread every scribbled note and written memorandum that McKay Wallace and Granger Mitchell made during their conversations with Celia and Dominique. I haven't found anything interesting, per se, but there are plenty of things in Celia's files that I find objectionable."

"Like?" Fred asks.

"Like, she refers to the people associated with Tango as *the ethnics*...and she says the organization is full of doctors, lawyers, and Indian chiefs...and she refers to Gretchen's husband as *the boy*...stuff like that. Those phrases are everywhere."

"Great. Not only are we're looking for The Body, now we're looking for an Indian chief."

"Not me, I'm looking forward to a physical therapy session and massage."

"I can handle the massage," Ted calls out to her.

"A massage and foreplay are two very different things, Detective Brothers."

Ted groans.

Fred laughs.

Penny moans.

DC

Felicity Ferraro spent a restless night banging up against the little elbows, knees, and feet of her brood. She pulls the last of her little ones from her king-size bed with an excited, "Come on. Come on. You need to finish packing. Mommy is way ahead of you slack-abouts," she pulls her stuffed suitcase from the floor, flops it onto the bed, with a "Whoomph," to the delighted squeal of her children.

On the way to the airport, a mother joins her kids in song, regales them with the things they will do on vacation, and hands them crackers and drinks, "Nibble and sip quickly. You can't bring those onto the plane." An hour later, Felicity pulls her SUV to a curb, places a kiss on the forehead of each of her unconscious children, releases them without word to the custody of a family member. She waits until the plane lifts off, then drives from the airport in tears.

DC Correctional Treatment Facility

Attorney Ferraro is already seated when her client is brought into the meeting room. She waits through the unshackling, the seating, and the re-shackling before speaking.

"I think..."

"Don't say a fucking word, Felicity."

She crosses her arms and leans back.

"I heard you got a promotion. I heard you've bought yourself some time with the Gang of Eight. I heard you've sent our children away."

"How?"

"Shut. The. Fuck. Up."

Felicity remains deathly still.

"Where are our children, Felicity?"

"With my family in Dublin."

Paul shakes his head. "Nope." Paul smiles wide. "**My** children are not on their way to Dublin."

"What have you done?"

"I took what's mine."

"Paul..."

"Shut the fuck up. You need to be put in your place, Felicity. You made a unilateral decision for our children. You need to be punished for that. You **think** you are calling the shots—with me, with our kids, hell, you **think** you are The Face of an international crime organization." He lets out a maniacal laugh. "You **think** you were hand-selected by The Body. You don't even know who The Body is."

"What?"

"Turner Rodgers is **not** The Body." Paul remains silent for several minutes. He enjoys the multitude of changes that cross his wife's face, her beautiful, albeit strained face.

"Who is The Body?"

"The Body is every single person you encounter. So, watch your step and your mouth, wifey." He gives her another minute then says, "Get your ass over here, give your husband a kiss, and lift your skirt."

Felicity looks at the door, "I can't, it's against the rules."

"**I** fucking make the rules, Felicity. Now, wrap your pussy around my dick."

Loose ends.

Layne Osterman has spent two days at Sergeant Noone's firing range, near Blue Marsh Lake, eighty miles northwest of Philly. She's made herself 'one' with her sniper rifle and 'one' with an assassin's headspace. On her way to the Camaro she sets contingencies for the immediate period of time after the mission, "Sarge, I may need a place to go low for a while."

"You found my place once, you can find it again. Good luck, Ranger. Don't forget to make the call before the shot, 'Geronimo', they yell in unison.

Layne spends the next two days in Philly doing reconnaissance. On the day of the hit, she makes a call, "It's on." At 3 PM, she drives past Pennsylvania Hospital just as two paramedics pull their ambulance from the bay. "First emergency call of the day—enjoy it." She drives two miles east from the hospital, pulls into a shopping mall parking lot, and listens to emergency calls on a police scanner app she downloaded onto her smartphone. At 10 PM, she listens to 9-1-1 dispatch send the EMTs to a call. She plugs the address into her GPS and drives to the location. "Enjoy this call, too, guys, it's the last one of your lives."

Layne Osterman, recently promoted sniper of The Realm waits a half-mile back from the patient's house. Within minutes, sirens and lights cut through the night, announcing the EMTs still have a live one. The ambulance is just gaining speed when it nears her. She sets her sights on the driver, whispers "Geronimo," and takes the shot. The ambulance swerves left-right-left, jumps the curb, travels a few hundred feet, and crashes sideways into a tree. She waits for movement inside the driver's cab. There is none. From the corner of her eye, she sees the back door of the ambulance swing open, and an EMT hop out. He rounds the corner toward the driver's side, quickly realizes he can't open that door, so he heads toward the passenger side. Layne whispers, "Geronimo," and takes the shot. The assassin spends the next few-seconds eyeing the lifeless bodies of two men. As she walks away, she whispers, "Shift's over."

Drexel Hill

Penny is tucked onto the recliner, where she intends to stay for the duration. She is hurting and exhausted from her physical therapy session, still she has enough energy to banish the men from the den. They take refuge in the kitchen and are enjoying a bowl of cereal when a knock comes at the front door. Ted races to it and pulls it open.

"It's midnight, Landry," he whispers.

"Yes, sir," the young officer says, "but you'll want to know what happened earlier."

Ted steps back, "Come on into the kitchen," he whispers as they move past a sleeping Penny. "Can I get you anything?"

"No, thank you, Detective. I'm off shift, so I'll be heading home. I'd still be on the clock, though, if I caught the last call, sir. Two EMTs were killed over on Frist."

"Accident?"

"No, sir. A shooting."

"You said two EMTs were killed?"

"Yes, sir. Last I heard there was talk about a sniper."

Fred is on his feet, "Officer Landry, wait here, please." The Detective goes to the den where sleeping Penny is kicked back. He quietly rummages through his overstuffed duffle, hoping he has better luck this time. He finds what he's looking for and heads back to the kitchen.

"Officer, any chance the paramedics names are, Robert Arsenault and Adam Booker?"

The young officer is nodding before he answers, "Yes. That's right, sir."

Ted taps Landry on the shoulder, "Go home, Officer. Don't discuss this little gathering with anyone, is that clear?"

"Yes, Detective."

"And Landry—"

"Yes, sir."

"I won't forget all the help you've been."

"Yes, sir."

Fred barely contains his, "Holy fuck," until the door closes behind Landry. Someone showed up here to finish the job on Penny, and most likely to take you out at the same time, probably to grab some files on the Brettenvue women, and now someone took out the two EMTs who worked on Paul Ferraro in the woods."

"You've said this before Fred, but it's worth repeating—someone is cutting a few loose ends."

"Yeah."

Did you call to chit-chat?

Mike arrived at Stacy Remington's townhouse late the night before. His visit was explained to Mathis Reynolds as a side trip to check on his friend's condition, post-concussion. When the RFI specialist enters the kitchen the next morning, he hears the click of a door. "The secret panel I've heard about," he peeks into the pantry, "the grieving husband must have…" he stops himself, "none of my business what a grieving husband must have been doing." He shakes his head, then busies himself with the task of setting coffee and rummaging for things to make French toast.

The aromas from Mike's efforts pull Mathis back through the pantry wall, "Something smells worthy of eating," he smiles.

"A little pay back for your hospitality, Mr. Reynolds."

"None needed, and it's Mathis. I hope I didn't disturb you earlier."

"I apologize for interrupting your…" Mike throws a look at a framed picture of Stacy sitting on the kitchen table.

"I try to find a few minutes alone with my thoughts of Stacy. Truth be told, I'm very glad you are all here. Your presence dictates that my grieving be measured. It's the right way of things." Mathis pulls a long sip of coffee and eyes the plate of French toast heading his way. "Now, if breakfast is as tasty as it smells, then I am very glad you are all here." A genuine roll of bliss crosses the man's face at his first bite, "There is something different in these. I taste sugar and cinnamon, as is expected, but there is something else." He takes another bite, "Do I taste pepper?"

"The tiniest pinch of white pepper, yes. A chef told me that whatever flavor you're going for, it will be enhanced by adding a pinch of the opposite flavor."

"Does this chef have a name?"

"Annie," Mike's smile gives *it* away.

"Annie is your partner?"

"She is. She's a brilliant woman…"

Mathis cuts him off—and changes subjects, "You were there that night?"

Mike nods, knowing what night Mathis is referring to, "I was."

The widower quickly eyes Stacy's photo, "I don't know exactly what happened out there, but as I told Manuel, the only way Stacy would have lived through that night is if she wasn't in that room with Granger. The minute she realized he was in danger, she—"

"Is that Annie's French Toast?" Leavy practically pants.

"It's a slice of Heaven is what it is," Mathis moans, as his fork finds his mouth.

Before Leavy's butt finds a seat, she receives a call from Fred, "I'm just sitting for breakfast, Fred. Mike just made Annie's French Toast."

"Talk freely. I want the ears privy."

"He stopped in to check on me and ended up staying the night. I think he's heading into DC to see his future father-in-law."

"Tell him he's a glutton for punishment."

"Hey, Mike, Fred says you're a glutton for punishment."

"A man's gotta do what a man's gotta do," Mike retorts.

"So, Fred, did you call to chit-chat?"

"I think I left some files. Can you take a look around?"

"When I'm done eating. Bye." Leavy takes her first bite, moans in ecstasy and says, "Fred thinks he might have left a couple files around. I'll go scavenging, but not until I've had my fill of this. So good, Mike."

"Is Fred expected to be away long?" Mathis asks.

"Maybe a couple of days. He's working an angle on the assassination…" Leavy cuts her sentence short, and sheepishly looks toward Mathis, "Oh, I'm sorry, Mathis, I shouldn't have said…"

He reaches across the table and squeezes Leavy's hand, "Talk freely. I already know Stacy's gone, and I know who killed her.

Now, if you will excuse me, I need to head to the office." With that, Mathis Reynolds, lawyer by trade, wall-walker by design, escapes through the pantry.

Drexel Hill

Fred and Ted are on their way back from dropping Stacy's GPS tracked vehicle at the Carriage House.

"You want The Realm to think you're there?"

"I don't want them to think I'm with Penny. They've already tried to kill her twice, so the contract on her is most likely a 'don't stop' order. If that's the case, there's gonna be another attempt. I'm thinking your little log cabin is going to be seeing some gunplay soon. When they show up, they'll be expecting you and Penny to be there. They won't be expecting me and Mike to be there."

Go back!

Mike passes Eli on his way out of the townhouse. Introductions between the two are kept short, “Heard a lot about you, Eli. I wish I could hang for a while, but I’ve got a meeting with my future father-in-law and I do not want to keep him waiting.” Mike pulls Leavy in for a hug, then gets escorted to his car by Manuel.

“You sure you’re gonna be alright by yourself?” Mike presses.

“I’m not by myself. Leavy is a former federal agent, and Mathis and Eli are pretty much always around. And I’m waiting to hear back from our boss. He’s making a plan to get Leavy and me out of DC later today.”

Mike nods, “Okay, then. Call if you need me.”

Drexel Hill

Penny passes through the kitchen on her way for a shower. “Holler if you need me,” Ted says—Ted always says. Minutes later, the men run toward her screams. Ted pushes open the door.

Fred follows him in, “Penny, what’s wrong?”

The woman is standing in the middle of the floor, dripping wet, and holding a towel across very little. "Doctor, lawyer, Indian chief. Doctor, lawyer, Indian chief. Celia's words. They are describing people in The Realm. There's a doctor, a lawyer, and the Indian chief probably refers to the Army Ranger. They are trained paratroopers. Paratroopers always call 'Geronimo!' on the way out of a plane."

Fred bolts from the bathroom and grabs Leavy's military printouts from his duffle. He scans, he scans, he scans. He finds it. Eli Reynolds, Ranger medic.

Fred grabs his cell and calls Mike, "WHERE ARE YOU?"

"Heading your way."

"GO BACK! GO BACK! ELI REYNOLDS IS PART OF THIS. HE'S GONNA TAKE LEAVY!"

Mike spins around and races back.

Fred calls Manuel. No answer.

Fred calls Leavy. No answer.

Fred calls Mike, "No one at the townhouse is answering my calls."

"Fuck, fuck, fuck!" Mike says as he pulls up to Stacy Remington's townhouse. "The Mercedes that was at the curb when I left a few minutes ago is gone, and the front door is open. Stay on the line. I'm going in."

Mike enters the quiet townhouse. There is evidence of a struggle in the living room, mostly kicked back rugs and a knocked over lamp. Mike hears something upstairs. He moves purposefully, but quietly. He picks up his pace when he hears a moan. He finds Manuel on the floor of Stacy's bedroom.

"Fred, Manuel's shot, he's down. Get help."

Mike rolls Manuel, checks vitals, starts CPR. Talking himself through it, "Thirty compressions, two breaths, thirty compressions, two breaths, thirty compressions…"

MedStar Health

Fred, Ted, and Penny arrive at the hospital several hours later to find a barely-holding-it-together-Mike and an urgently-pacing-John who looks to Fred and shakes his head.

Fred falls back against a wall and lowers to the floor.

Ted gives him a minute, then kneels next to him, "Fred. Leavy is gone, tell me what to do to help find her."

Fred flips his switch and pulls himself up. He walks to John, "Leavy. We have to find Leavy."

John rights himself. He approaches Mike and puts his hand onto his shoulders, "Leavy. We have to find Leavy."

Mike and John stand silently as Fred makes a call.

"Rocco. Rocco. I'm sorry.
It's Manuel. He's gone."

The End

More to come …

Please enjoy the teaser for my next book in the series, *Resolve…*

RESOLVE

THE CANDIDATE

--- PULLING THREADS ---

Book Thirteen

SHERYLL O'BRIEN

Two lovers are gone.

One was shot and left for dead.
One was taken against her will.

ABOUT THE AUTHOR

She is not dead.

Sheryll O'Brien crafts characters without constraints. She tells them who they are, then let's them show her better versions of themselves. She gives them life and they live it beyond her wildest dreams.

Sheryll is a lifelong resident of Worcester, Massachusetts, where she is wife to the most supportive husband ever, and mother of two adult daughters, one who refuses to leave her home and the other who refuses to tell her where she lives. Of most significance, she is MammyGrams to the sweetest six-year-old, Hadley.

Sheryll worked several years in the fundraising community of Worcester County, writing grants for non-profit organizations. She began writing for her own pleasure after surviving brain surgery and breast cancer. Happily, for her fanbase of family and friends-—she is not dead.

If you have enjoyed reading my book, I would very much appreciate you taking a few minutes to write a review and post that review on amazon.com and goodreads.com.

The opinion of readers can help prospective readers make a purchasing decision.

To learn more, please visit my website, www.pullingthreadsnovella.com subscribe to my blog for updates on future projects.

I would absolutely love to hear from my readers, you can email me at,

pullingthreadsnovella@gmail.com

www.ingramcontent.com/pod-product-compliance
Lightning Source LLC
LaVergne TN
LVHW010057110826
845155LV00028B/384

* 9 7 8 1 9 3 9 3 5 1 3 2 6 *